THE DEADLY SHADOW

In the winter of 1888, a gang led by notorious desperado Taw Johnson arrives at a small ranch near the town of Chinook. Cathy Clemens is recently married, but temporarily alone on the ranch, and Johnson makes the fateful decision to carry her off. When her husband John returns, he swears vengeance and sets off in pursuit, coldly picking the men off one by one. Against all the odds, the impressionable Cathy finds herself attracted to Johnson — and ever more alienated by her husband's unrelentingly cruel behaviour . . .

N

PAUL BEDFORD

THE DEADLY SHADOW

Complete and Unabridged

LINFORD
Leicester

First published in Great Britain in 2016 by
Robert Hale Limited
An imprint of The Crowood Press
Wiltshire

First Linford Edition
published 2018
by arrangement with
The Crowood Press
Wiltshire

A catalogue record for this book is available
from the British Library.

ISBN 978–1–4448–3820–6

Published by
F. A. Thorpe (Publishing)
Anstey, Leicestershire

Set by Words & Graphics Ltd.
Anstey, Leicestershire
Printed and bound in Great Britain by
T. J. International Ltd., Padstow, Cornwall

This book is printed on acid-free paper

1

It was the premature onset of winter in that year of 1888 that finally drove the band of scavengers across the Canadian border and down into Montana Territory. Its harsh effects always came unpleasantly early in the high latitudes. There was, of course, another reason for their departure. The lawless, brutalized bunch had stirred up more than enough trouble in Queen Victoria's lands and it hadn't all gone their way. They had originally numbered twenty riders, but after a bruising encounter with a North-West Mounted Police patrol, that figure had dropped to fifteen. Weeks later, the outcome of the vicious fight near Moose Jaw in Saskatchewan still rankled with some of the men.

'It just ain't fair, I tells you,' muttered Kenny Packard angrily, as he massaged his aching thigh. The cold weather badly affected his partially healed flesh wound. 'There never used to be any law up there and now it's swarming with bastard redcoats. Where the hell do we go next time we need to lay low?'

His nearest crony regarded him askance. 'We weren't exactly laying low. And in any case, I seem to recollect it was you on point that day. If you hadn't been drinking Who-Hit-John all morning, we wouldn't have ridden smack into that god damned Mountie patrol in the first place.'

'Nah, nah,' piped up another man displaying all the features of a simpleton. 'It weren't called 'First Place'. It was something else ending in Jaw or Paw. You mark my words!'

'I'll mark your poxy face in a minute,' responded the second speaker with casual belligerence and so the exchange went on and on.

Some yards behind them, two men rode companionably knee-to-knee, all the while keeping their voices low.

'For pity's sake, Taw, why don't we

cut loose of these morons? They haven't got an ounce of sense between them!'

Taw Johnson regarded the other man amiably as he formulated a response. Johnson possessed a big open face with moderately intelligent eyes that seemed to sparkle when he was in conversation with someone that he liked. In fact, everything about him was big. Big boned, strongly muscled and barrel-chested, he rode a massive horse that had to be at least seventeen hands high. Glancing briefly at his bickering men, he then returned his full attention to his lieutenant, Clay Bassett.

'Because when it comes to gunplay, as it *always* seems to, it pays to have plenty of bodies around to absorb the bullets. Besides, that fool Packard unwittingly got one thing right. Times are changing. There's more and more folks heading West and that'll mean more lawmen. It won't just be Canada that'll run us out. Hell, I hear tell that Montana's going to be made a state soon. Then we won't be able to move for marshals and sheriffs and stock detectives and even god damn Pinkertons. It makes me want to vomit, just thinking on it!'

Bassett, lean and twitchy, hadn't heard his boss talk like this before and he didn't like it one little bit. 'So where does that leave the likes of us? Living by our wits and guns is all we know.'

Johnson drew in a deep breath and consciously relaxed a little. Before continuing, he checked around to make sure that they hadn't been overheard. As expected, the other twelve members of his gang that were visible showed no apparent interest in their two leaders. They were otherwise occupied, either bickering with each other or dozing in the saddle as only those born to the life could manage.

'I've never been to Mexico, but I hear tell that the law can be bought cheap down there. And you get some real warmth, which has to be better than this,' he added, instinctively pulling his jacket tighter around him.

Bassett couldn't hide his surprise. 'So what's your plan? Because you always seem to have one.'

The big man chuckled appreciatively. 'I figure we learn from the Apache and Comanche and other wild tribes. Apparently they take whatever they can get in these United States of Assholes and sell it over the border. Except that whereas they also loot and pillage the Mexicans as well, we'll keep our noses clean down there. That way we won't wear out our welcome. That's what we got wrong up north.'

His sidekick's eyes were like saucers as he took all this in. 'Sounds like you've got it all thought out, but just how far is it to Mexico, anyhow?'

For the first time doubt appeared on Johnson's bluff features. 'The truth is I don't rightly know, but as far as everyone else is concerned we just keep heading south, which will make those simpletons think it's downhill all the way. And one thing I do know,' he added fiercely, 'is that we're going to take everything in our path that's not nailed down and God help anyone who tries to stop us, because I've had a belly full of being poor!'

★ ★ ★

Cathy Clemens regarded her husband with mixed feelings as he hitched his horse to the small flatbed wagon. Although the young woman had only been married to John for six months, she viewed the prospect of being separated from him for a couple of days with nervous pleasure. His patient, mostly kind and yet strangely controlling presence had begun to grate on her a little and there was a long, hard winter ahead. God knew how she was going to put up with him through the cold, dark days. She told herself that it would be different when they had a child to dilute the relationship, but as yet there was no sign of that happening.

As he glanced over at her standing in the entrance to the two-roomed log

6

cabin, she flushed guiltily. Those penetrating eyes of his seemed to bore right through her, reading her thoughts in the process. She favoured him with a bright smile, hoping to deflect any awkward questions. Only after tightening the last strap to his satisfaction, did he move over to her.

John Clemens cut an imposing figure in his buckskin jacket. Six feet tall with a lean, sinewy physique, he projected an image of competence . . . and possibly something else besides. When driven to anger, an indefinable aura of menace came over him. Cathy had only witnessed it once and didn't care to again.

'Remember what I said,' he instructed firmly. 'Stay close to the cabin and bar the door and windows as soon as it falls dark. And keep hold of that Winchester at all times.'

'Even when I'm in bed?' she queried frivolously, only to be rewarded with a dark scowl that immediately crushed her spirit. Deep down she felt that he meant well, but she was tiring of his repeated instructions.

Rather than responding with some light banter as she might have wished, John instead took in the surrounding landscape with a great sweeping gesture. Their cabin sat in splendid isolation on a lush meadow in northern Montana. Low, gently undulating hills spread out in all directions, save to the north where there was a great stand of Ponderosa pine trees. A newly constructed corral along with a substantial barn showed that there had been a fair few dollars spent on the spread recently. On a thick section of timber nailed above the cabin entrance, the words *New Haven* were carved in bold letters, hinting that someone was quite possibly seeking exactly that.

'This is untamed country and you're going to be all on your lonesome until I get back,' he replied more harshly than he had intended. 'I know the redskins have been pacified and you'll likely not see another soul, but I don't want you taking any chances, you hear?'

Cathy's beautiful features registered hurt as she nodded silently. He sighed and consciously moderated his tone. He knew full well that his concern for her led to his being overpowering at times and he also knew why he did it. She sometimes seemed so innocent to the ways of the world, whilst he had seen more bloodshed in his time than any man should. There was also the fact that he took very literally the word 'obey' as uttered in the marriage vows.

'Once I buy the stock and take on some hired men, things will be different, you'll see. I just don't want any harm to come to you, is all. By rights you should be coming to Chinook with me.'

Cathy shook her head in a surprising display of determination. 'You've put a lot of money and effort into these buildings. We can't just abandon them, even for only two days. And you have to be the one to go into town to buy the supplies. They'd be too heavy for me to handle.'

John looked her up and down attentively, as though he was storing a vision of her away in his mind. She really was stunningly attractive. Even the drab work clothes couldn't hide her enviable figure. Her flawless skin had yet to suffer from the gruelling winters that he knew were ahead of them and he suddenly felt great warmth for her. It was just a pity that he couldn't always show it. As all too often with John Clemens, action took the place of words. Abruptly taking hold of his young wife, he gripped her strongly and planted a fierce kiss on her full lips.

She recoiled slightly under his heavily enthusiastic assault, before returning the pressure. Not for the first time, it occurred to her that it would be so nice if he could just display a little more tenderness. Then again, had she known the full truth of his past deeds, she quite probably wouldn't have even married him!

As the wagon rattled off along the almost non-existent trail towards the frontier settlement of Chinook, Cathy drew in a steadying breath and watched impatiently until her husband was completely out of sight. Only then did she let out a little whoop of joy and leap into the open, pirouetting a full 360 degrees. The silence was total and the reality of her temporary solitude held no fears. Instead, her heart beat fiercely as a surge of anticipation flowed through her. She had been looking forward to this moment for days. The prospect of luxuriating in the tin tub full of hot water, without John's judgemental eyes on her, would be worth all the considerable effort of carrying and heating the liquid.

Full of anticipation, the young woman turned back towards the south-facing entrance and just happened to glance over to the distant pine trees. What she saw caused her to freeze with shock. The very faintest wisp of smoke drifted across the treetops and was gone. For long moments she stared anxiously at the spot, but no more appeared and she soon began to doubt its very existence. Perhaps it had just been the treetops shimmying in the breeze or maybe even smoke from her own fire drifting skywards.

Finally Cathy shook her head and consciously dismissed her fears. She had work to do before she could enjoy her longed-for treat and no optical illusion was going to spoil it for her!

2

Taw Johnson sipped the hot coffee with exaggerated relish as he surveyed his surroundings. He and most of his men were lounging around in a clearing in the trees, eating and drinking. They had covered a lot of miles the day before and so he was cutting them some slack, before moving on into open country. Always on edge, Clay Bassett had drifted on ahead to reconnoitre and it wasn't long before he returned with a gleam of anticipation in his eyes.

'We got us a nice little homestead waiting beyond these pines, Taw. There's a fire burning so it's occupied, but from the lack of horses there can't be many people to give us trouble.'

Johnson's eyes lit up with fierce anticipation and suddenly it wasn't just the coffee that was warming his insides. Raiding was in his blood. 'Well, whatever's down there is about to get a change of owner.' Tossing the dregs into the fire, he threw the tin cup at the nearest man and clapped his hands enthusiastically. 'Saddle up, boys. We've got business elsewhere!'

The wood, so filled with birdsong, suddenly rang with the excited cries of seasoned looters and pillagers, as all thoughts of coffee and beans were forgotten.

★ ★ ★

Cathy Clemens eased her naked body into the steaming water and uttered a great sigh of satisfaction. The tub was facing the open door, so that she could gaze out on the lush grassland. With the hot liquid shielding her from the chill air, her sense of peace was absolute. She couldn't remember the last time that she had felt so completely relaxed. For once, all and any chores were to be undertaken in her own good time, with no chiding husband lurking around to spoil it for her. Very slowly, the heat worked its magic. Her eyelids began to close, shutting out the primitive surroundings. The only possible thing likely to interrupt her tranquillity was the inevitable cooling of the water.

The pounding of many hoofs around the cabin was so totally unexpected that the drowsy young woman violently jerked with surprise and slid under the surface. So it was that the first rider to swing past the entrance saw only an unoccupied tub. Gasping and spluttering, Cathy came back up for air and heard the excited voices of many men as they reined in around her home.

Although she couldn't possibly have realized it, the moment that would define her future was upon her. She could either freeze to the spot and accept everything that befell her or she could show some real grit and refuse to tolerate the frightening intrusion. Instinctively, Cathy Clemens chose the latter. Leaping out of the water, she slammed the door shut and slipped the solid wooden bar into place, mere seconds before one of the intruders reached it. Even as a heavy boot slammed ineffectually against the rough-cut timber, she raced back into the bedroom.

Stark naked and trembling with a mixture of fear and anger, there were two immediate requirements on her mind: modesty and defence. Still dripping wet, the young woman hastily slipped into a calico dress and then reached for the Winchester that her husband had been so insistent on her having. As her left hand closed around its comforting fore stock, she heard a chuckle from outside the open window. Spinning around, Cathy was confronted by the head and shoulders of a complete stranger. He had obviously seen everything, because the unsettling mixture of both a smile and a suggestive leer registered on his broad face.

Desperately working the under-lever of the rifle, she then vaguely aimed from the hip and fired. With a stunning crash the weapon discharged, although with what result she had no idea. Wreathed in sulphurous powder smoke and with her ears ringing painfully, she closed and bolted the single shutter. The bedroom was plunged into darkness and as if in reaction, she began to shiver with cold. The only light now came from the one open window in the main room. After pumping up another cartridge, Cathy carefully padded across the dirt floor to secure it.

Before she could get there, a fusillade of shots rang out directly beyond the window and bullets smashed into various timbers around her. As vicious splinters narrowly missed her, she shrieked involuntarily and dropped into a crouch. Never before in her life had she been shot at!

Taw Johnson's excellent reflexes came into play and he leapt aside from the window in the nick of time. As Cathy's bullet sped off into the void, he watched as the window shutter slammed fast. With the vision of her voluptuous figure imbedded in his mind, Johnson shook his head in admiration. Then, as a volley of shots rattled off around the corner, his intrigue swiftly turned to anger.

'Stop that god damned shooting!' he bellowed out at his bewildered followers. 'Jed, what did you see when you passed the entrance?'

'An empty tub was all, boss,' responded that individual.

Johnson scratched his bristly chin with grubby fingers as he pondered the unforeseen situation. Then he broke into a broad smile. When something seemed too good to be true it usually was, but on this occasion it actually appeared as though his ship had come in.

'Seems to me there's just the one lone pilgrim in there. No sense in risking our lives storming the place,' he announced somewhat theatrically. Then, raising his voice for Cathy's benefit, he added, 'So I reckon we'll set the place afire. It'll be the warmest we've been this month.

Fetch some kindling, boys.'

The chill that came over Cathy Clemens no longer related to her damp body. The prospect of being burnt to death filled her with abject horror. Surely no one would make good on such a threat. Manically clutching her rifle, the terrified young woman listened intently to the muted sounds outside. None of the intruders came near the remaining open window, but the gunfire had served its purpose and she too kept well clear. Then a whiff of wood smoke drifted through the shutter and her worst fear was confirmed.

From outside, the same man's voice sounded off again. 'Pile it on, boys. It's good and dry. We're going to have quite a blaze.'

Before long, Cathy could hear the crackling sound of wood burning and she began to choke on the thick smoke that flowed in through the open window. Her cabin was on fire and there was no one to help her. Momentarily she cursed John's absence and then the only thing on her mind was to get out of the doomed building. Scrabbling over to the door, she heaved the crossbar out of its brackets and yelled out, 'I'm coming out. For pity's sake, don't shoot me!'

With her eyes streaming, Cathy yanked open the door and burst out into the cool crisp air. At that point, two things happened that only added to her distress. Her feet were kicked out from under her and as she hit the ground with bruising force, the Winchester was torn from her grasp. Desperately, she sucked air into her voided lungs, but it was some moments before she was able to focus on her surroundings. And then she got yet another very unwelcome shock.

A band of grimy, rough looking men was scattered around the clearing in front of the cabin and all eyes were fixed on her. The terrified young woman abruptly realized that her thin dress had ridden high up her shapely thighs. Hastily, she dragged the material down over her knees, but that action only seemed to encourage the watching ruffians.

'By Christ, she's a real peach,' one of them muttered and then en masse they closed in around her. Dreadfully aware of what was about to happen, all she could do was stare in horror at their repulsive, brutalized features.

Then a voice that she recognized roared out, 'All right, all right. Break it up or I'll start smashing heads.'

Two men were dragged out of the way and a big, powerful individual suddenly provided her with a faint glimmer of hope. Then she recognized him as the man she had shot at and her heart sank again.

'Yeah, that's right.' He sniggered. 'You missed!'

Barging to the forefront of his men, Taw Johnson reached down and seized her arms. Seemingly effortlessly, he heaved her upright and then quite blatantly looked her up and down.

'My, my. You're a real honey, aren't

you?' he remarked throatily.

Something snapped inside Cathy's skull. She might be cold, desperately afraid and friendless, but no big oaf was going to treat her like a piece of meat. Tearing her right arm free, she planted a stinging slap across her assailant's face.

'Take your hands off me, you pig. My husband and his men will be back soon and they'll make you pay dearly for this!'

Johnson appeared not to even notice the sudden blow, but her words stirred his curiosity. 'Just how many men have you got working this spread? There can't be but a few, because if it was me, I wouldn't leave you all alone out here for even five minutes.'

Cathy stared at him with a mixture of surprise and loathing. It had just dawned on her that the cabin wasn't actually on fire and the cunning deception rankled.

'John's got ten riders and they're all armed to the teeth!' she declared angrily. Even to her the heated reply rang hollow, a fact that she realized as soon as the words were out of her mouth.

The big man didn't attempt to disguise his amusement. 'Well, is that a fact? Hell, if I'd known this place was so well defended, I'd have stayed up in Canada.' He suddenly thrust his head forward, so that they were almost nose-to-nose. 'What's your name, girl?'

Resentment again flared up within her. 'Cathy. Cathy Clemens. And I'm no girl!'

Johnson blatantly glanced down at her barely concealed cleavage. 'Oh, I can see that.' A crazy idea had suddenly entered his head. 'If all your gun-toting ranch hands are about to descend on us, we'd better get moving. Fix yourself up with some warm clothes. You're coming with us!'

That declaration got more than just Cathy in a lather. The watching raiders began to lick their lips at the prospect. And yet Clay Bassett immediately shook his head in dismay. 'I don't reckon that's a good idea, boss. Whores in a town's one thing, but to bring one along on the trail with us can only cause trouble. Let's just all have her here, take what we want and torch the place. That's what we've always done in the past.'

Johnson stared at him long and hard in stony silence. He knew full well that his right hand man spoke good sense. And yet . . . Cathy looked so good she made him ache inside. He had never ever possessed a woman like her and quite likely never would . . . unless he took this one chance. Right or wrong, his mind was made up. Hardening his heart, he responded to Bassett's well-meaning counsel and yet even as he spoke, the outlaw leader knew that he was making a mistake.

'At least you got one word right, Clay. *Boss*, because that's what I am. And until that changes, I'll make the decisions. And this ain't the past anymore. We're for Mexico and new beginnings, remember?'

Ignoring the visible hurt on the other man's face, Johnson turned to his prisoner and almost as an afterthought, unleashed a lazy backhand slap. The blow was enough to knock Cathy off her feet and brought tears to her eyes.

'Now, *lady*,' the outlaw leader snarled. 'You need to realize that I ain't asking anymore. I'm telling. So go get your things together and keep your hands off any more firearms!'

She stared at him dumbly for a long moment, before slowly getting to her feet and returning indoors. Clay Bassett watched in silence as his boss moved off to oversee the looting. He had more than just bitter rejection on his mind. He was trying very hard to recall where he had heard the name John Clemens before.

The low sun had barely moved across the sky before the scavengers mounted up. They had removed every scrap of food and every item of value from the cabin. Over her strongest objections,

Cathy found herself riding double in unpleasantly close proximity with the bear-like Johnson.

'We'll steal a horse for you when we can,' he stated. 'Although for myself I'm more than happy with this arrangement.'

'I thought we were going to torch the cabin,' remarked Bassett sourly, eliciting a horrified gasp from its owner.

Johnson, who was acutely aware of the woman's supple body pressing against his, had other things on his mind and was in an unusually good humour.

'Nah, I was just funning. This man Clemens is going to be hurting bad when he finds out someone's took his woman. Might as well leave him something for the winter, ha ha. After all,' he added, pointing to the name plaque above the cabin's open door, 'looks to me like he's trying to put some bad times behind him.' With that he gestured south and bellowed out, 'Let's ride,' and they did.

Not for one moment did it occur to him that 'this man Clemens' might actually decide to pursue such a large gang of desperados. And it was also left to the deep thinking Clay Bassett to ponder over the rather fanciful thought that New Haven might just possibly refer to the New Haven Arms Company of Connecticut: former producer of the revolutionary Henry repeating rifle.

3

John Clemens had spent an unsettled night in a rough and ready rooming house, which was all the town of Chinook possessed in the way of accommodation unless he had been prepared to surrender himself to one of the local whores. As on so many occasions before in such surroundings, his past life came back to haunt him in the form of vivid dreams. After waking up drenched in sweat, it had been a relief to dip his head in the water trough outside. Thankfully, 'two bits' worth of strong coffee and a fried breakfast set him up to face the new day and he was soon back on the trail, his wagon loaded with essential supplies for the winter.

The prospect of rejoining his young wife excited him, even after such a brief separation. He was well aware of just how attractive she was and of how very lucky he had been to find her on his trip back East. Unfortunately, that knowledge frequently led to feelings of insecurity, which manifested themselves in boorish and controlling behaviour. Even as he rattled his way back to New Haven, the hunter turned rancher vowed, not for the first time, to change his ways and improve his relationship with her.

The moment he set eyes on the cabin, Clemens knew that something was amiss. The building's only door was wide open and a wisp of smoke trickled lazily up from just beyond the far side of the structure. Resisting the urge to charge forward hell for leather, he instead reined in and reached down below the wagon's bench seat. From a long leather scabbard, he withdrew his meticulously maintained Sharps model 1874 rifle and cocked the hammer. Only then did he cautiously roll on towards his home. Instinctively, Clemens knew that Cathy was gone, because at no time did he call out her name.

With his heart pounding fit to burst, he prowled around his property, reading the signs and piecing together what had happened. The large number of horse tracks indicated a sizeable raiding party, but the hoofs were shod so it was unlikely that Indians were involved. The leafy fire, slightly removed from the wall, had been a ruse. The empty cartridge case on the floor of the bedroom showed that his wife had fought back, but the lack of any bloodstains suggested that he should have taught her better.

The enormity of the situation suddenly overwhelmed him and he burst out of the cabin. Why had he left her all alone in a relatively untamed wilderness? Angrily, he prowled up and down in front of the name plaque. The two optimistic words now seemed merely to taunt him; his new start smashed to pieces by a gang of low life scum. The thought of his young wife in their brutal clutches brought forth an outpouring of incandescent rage and for a few moments, he howled uncontrollably at the empty landscape like a demented wolf. Spittle flew from his lips as the veins in his neck bulged alarmingly.

Then, quite suddenly, his fury turned inward and crystallized like ice in his veins. Cathy Clemens belonged to him. She was his wife and therefore his property and what was his had rarely been easy to take. Therefore his course of action was quite obvious. Regardless of their over-whelming numbers, he would pursue the outlaws and reclaim her. Whether he would actually want her back after her inevitable debauchery was an issue he could not yet bring himself to consider.

Mind made up, John Clemens went about his necessary tasks in a calm and considered manner. From then on there would be no more emotional outbursts, because such things could get a man killed. First, he went back into the cabin. The only positive outcome of the raid was that the building had not been razed to the ground. Consequently, his hidden possessions remained intact and there would likely be a home to return to, *if* he got her back and if nobody else destroyed it just for the hell of it in his absence.

Just to the right of the fireplace, there was a section of wall panelling that under careful inspection intruded further into the room than would be expected, but was only noticeable if the outside dimensions were measured. Using his fingernails, he prized open a hinged portion and inspected the contents of the secret chamber. By far the largest item was a pair of saddle-bags, which he hoisted out and opened. In one compartment there was crammed a thick wad of dollar bills, accumulated during a decade of killing on the northern plains. At one time there had actually been a lot more, but building a ranch from scratch did not come cheap. His top lip curled with the makings of a sneer, at the knowledge of just what the raiders had missed.

Next out was a leather gun belt, complete with cartridges and a revolver wrapped in an oiled rag. A brief inspection satisfied him that the Schofield was in full working order. There was a very particular reason for him owning such a make of weapon. The latch on the top of the frame allowed it to be broken open and then all the spent cartridges ejected at once. This meant that it could be reloaded faster than any other revolver available, a feature that had come in very useful when its owner was 'jumped' by angry redskins. Such an occurrence had been a commonplace hazard for professional buffalo hunters and Clemens had often interspersed such work with some even more unsavoury activities!

The addition of two full bandoliers of Sharps cartridges and a razor-edged skinning knife left the concealed chamber completely empty. After carefully resealing it, Clemens arranged the various weaponry about his person, and headed for the door. He emerged from the cabin a changed man, with bandoliers criss-crossing his chest and the gun belt fitting snugly around his waist. And yet he was altered in far more than just appearance. Gone was the prospective small rancher and family man. There was a harder set to his strong jaw, whilst his eyes held the far away look of a man who spent a lot of time scrutinizing his surroundings. John Clemens was taking up where he left off and not for the first time he was hunting men!

After leading the horse and wagon into the barn, he helped himself to as many supplies as could be stuffed into his substantial saddle-bags. They included coffee, corn meal, flour, sugar, salt and beans. The fact that he was commencing a manhunt meant that there would be few fires so he also packed a good supply of beef jerky and pemmican. A drawtube spyglass and a supply of Lucifers in wax paper completed the list long since committed to memory.

Releasing his horse from the wagon harness, Clemens rubbed her down and allowed her feed and water before heaving on his saddle. He tied on a thick woollen blanket from under the wagon's bench seat and then it was time to leave. The outlaws had at least a day's start on him, but he had little doubt that he would overhaul them. It never occurred to him that it might be more sensible not to.

Without a backward glance at his once highly prized new home, the grim-faced hunter set off after his prey. Following such a large band was child's play. They had made no attempt to disguise their path, being quite obviously overconfident in their numbers and not expecting any pursuit. He gave no thought to what he was leaving behind. If he and Cathy did make it back to New Haven, any opportunistic squatters would be given very short shrift indeed. His blood was up and was very likely to remain so!

⋆　⋆　⋆

'God damn it all to hell! Who is it down there, Wild Bill Hickok his self?' The frustrated scavenger ducked under cover as more bullets ricocheted off the rocks.

'That don't seem possible,' another one responded in all seriousness. 'I seen him shot to death in Deadwood over ten years ago. That's known as a decade, you know,' he added helpfully.

'Shut up and lay down some fire, you morons,' Taw Johnson shouted angrily.

Back up the hillside, well out of harm's way, his prisoner gazed down on the unfolding drama with disbelief. It was hard to credit that they were going to all this trouble just to obtain a horse for her.

Since kidnapping Cathy Clemens, the gang had been resolutely heading due south. Their leader considered that to be a sure fire way of eventually reaching Mexico. They had passed the first night in the shelter of a stand of trees and it was here that Cathy expected her worst fears to come true. Amazingly, she had remained unsullied, although certainly not ignored. On their bear-like boss's instructions, his men had given her a wide berth, but that quite obviously didn't apply to him. Clutching her wrist in a vice like grip, Johnson had led her off into the undergrowth. Out of sight of the others, he had suddenly thrust her to the ground and shown every intention of assaulting her there and then.

She had no intention of submitting quietly, but suddenly found that loud and violent resistance was unnecessary, because the gang boss had unexpectedly backed off and merely stared at her long and hard.

'That's not the way it'll be,' he had finally remarked softly. 'You're too good for such.'

Despite her apparent reprieve, there was an intensity to his gaze that frightened the young woman. The very fact of being so stunningly attractive had enabled her to control most of her encounters with men in the past, even though they had usually come to nothing. It was a sad fact that she had

had little luck in her choice of men. What she now faced was something entirely different. She had never been the subject of such blatant animal desire, or so completely helpless in the face of it. And yet . . . for all her fear, a tiny part of her found the attention exciting and flattering. John had always seemed so controlled, as though all sensitivity had been crushed by the events of his earlier life.

She was jerked out of her thoughts and back to the present by a volley of gunfire from the rocks below her. Taw Johnson and his cronies were pouring a torrent of hot lead into a substantial cabin some one hundred yards away, but it seemed to be having little effect. The defenders continued to return an accurate fire. One man sustained a flesh wound and suddenly Johnson had had enough.

'Cease fire,' he bellowed. 'We carry on like this, we'll run out of cartridges and then *they'll* take all our horses!'

As the firing petered out on both

sides, he cupped his hands and hollered out, 'Hello, the cabin. There's really no need for any of this. All we want is the one horse . . . for a poor young lady who's come on bad times and found herself afoot. Only thing is, she ain't got any coin to speak of.'

They didn't have long to wait for a reply. The main door eased open and a grey head appeared.

'Go to hell, you thieving scroats! I never met a young lady yet who couldn't earn coin somehow. Anyone comes near our corral and we'll fill him full of lead. You hear?'

Clay Bassett shook his scrawny head and sighed, before scrambling over to join his boss. He was about to say what all the other men were thinking, but it gave him no pleasure.

'This won't answer, Taw. No good'll come of keeping that girl. It'll unsettle the others. Have her and be done with it.'

The colour began to rise in Johnson's thick neck as he glanced around at his men. They didn't look particularly unsettled to him, but there was no doubt that it was getting cold and he didn't take to being stood off by a bunch of no account settlers.

'They'll do as I say, not as I do,' he responded heatedly. 'Meantime, the girl needs a horse. Her riding double is starting to slow us down.' The big outlaw drew in a deep breath and roared down the wind to the cabin. 'Oh, I hear you, old man. But the thing is, we ain't leaving without a good horse and saddle. Just the one. I've kind of set my heart on it. So what's going to happen is this. We're going to keep you and your kin pinned down 'til nightfall. Then we're going to move in fast and pour coal oil all over your walls and burn every one of you sons of bitches to death. Then we'll take all of your animals and sell them to the army. How's that sound?'

Despite the tense situation, Bassett just had to chuckle. 'Coal oil'. That was a good one. As if any of them were carrying buckets of that stuff around.

Johnson's overblown threat obviously carried weight with the settlers, because after bare moments the grey head reappeared. This time the aggressive tone was much reduced. 'You're no better than the god damn Sioux. Send one man down here, unarmed. He picks out the one animal and then you all get off my property, pronto.'

A broad grin spread over Johnson's face. 'It'll be my pleasure, old friend,' he yelled back. 'And you have my deepest thanks.'

The old man's response resonated with bitterness and defeat. 'You know where you can stick that and I ain't your friend!'

Shortly after that last exchange, the scavengers extricated themselves from the rocks and took off. Cathy now had her own mount, but if she hoped that that additional freedom would allow her more chance to escape, she was to be disappointed. Her hands were fettered with rawhide and Taw Johnson had her reins looped around his left wrist at all times.

'You and I need to stick together,' he remarked softly as they jogged along. 'That way we can get to know each other better. We'll be in The Breaks shortly. Lay low there for a spell; just to make sure no one's on our back trail. We've upset a few folks lately and your man might be one of them. I've found it pays to be careful.'

In spite of the permanent simmering resentment that she felt at her kidnapping, Cathy's curiosity was aroused. 'What on earth is The Breaks?'

He stared at her in genuine amazement. 'You can't have lived in Montana for long, little lady.'

'I'd never been west of the Mississippi until John took me for his wife.' She hadn't meant for it to come out quite like that, but Johnson was sharp enough to have spotted it.

'Sounds to me like yours might not have been a marriage of equals,' he responded slyly, but when she lowered her head and failed to elaborate, he merely laughed and carried on. 'The Breaks is a vast stretch of land surrounding the Upper Missouri River. It might look interesting to some surveyor, but to people like us it's known as badlands. Hills, buttes, rock outcropping and forests make it a great place to hide out *and* it's pretty much deserted. Anyone tries coming to conclusions with us in there and they'll end up dead as a wagon tyre!'

⋆　⋆　⋆

John Clemens had ridden long and hard since leaving New Haven. By the late afternoon he had been able to make out the Bear Paw Mountains in the distance off to his right. He could not know of the various diversions that had delayed his prey, but somehow he sensed that he might be overhauling them. One man alone could always outpace a large group, regardless of interruptions.

As darkness came on, he and his horse were all but done in. Seething anger still consumed him, but the experienced hunter had sense enough to recognize that he needed to stop for the night. It was a long time since he had slept in the open and so it was a pleasant surprise when he suddenly came upon a substantial cabin along with other outbuildings. Lights were burning inside so he decided to chance his hand and test their hospitality. Care was needed, though. A man could end up in a cold hole in the ground, blundering into an unknown settlement in the dark. Dismounting, Clemens kept his hands clear of any weapons and led his horse forward until they were within easy hailing distance.

'Hello, the cabin,' he called out hopefully, completely ignorant of just how exactly his greeting replicated that of Taw Johnson's earlier in the day.

The response was chilling. As heavy boots thundered across bare floorboards, first the lights were doused and then the door was flung open. Clemens hadn't survived years on the frontier by luck alone. He was already in the dirt when the expected muzzle flash momentarily flared in the night. There was a blast of pressure as a rifle bullet flew over his head. Drawing and cocking his Schofield, he aimed directly at the dark shape in front of the cabin.

'If you or any other son of a bitch triggers a piece, you'll get to dying. You have my oath on that.' His warning was greeted with silence rather than more gunfire, which in itself was encouraging, so he continued with, 'You ain't right neighbourly. Why would that be?'

The solitary figure with the rifle retorted harshly, 'We ain't got any neighbours that we know of. Only robbing varmints that threaten to torch what's ours.'

Everything suddenly became clear in Clemens's mind. 'Well, I own a spread north of here a piece and those same varmints hit my place sometime yesterday. Took my wife, without even a 'by your leave'. I aim to get her back

. . . unless you figure on stopping me just for the hell of it,' he added sarcastically.

There was a sharp intake of breath as his words sank in and when his assailant next spoke it was with obvious embarrassment. 'Hell, mister. We thought you was one of them scum sucking outlaws come back to try their luck again. James, get those damn lamps lit. I almost made a terrible mistake here.'

Flickering light reappeared in the cabin and then a young man emerged, carrying a kerosene lamp. Its bright glow illuminated the scene and both father and son twitched with alarm at the sight of the revolver aimed directly at them. Clemens intentionally delayed a few seconds before holstering it and getting to his feet. With the full bandoliers draped around his torso, he was wholly aware of the effect his appearance might have on them.

'Hell's bells, mister,' remarked the young man. 'You're loaded for bear and no mistake.'

The unexpected visitor favoured him with a chill smile. 'This ain't no picnic I'm on. When I catch up with them fellas, there'll be some killing and I'll be the one doing it!'

The father gazed intently at him for a moment and then gestured towards the door. 'Please, you must come in and get warm. It's the least I can do after nearly shooting you and besides . . . I believe we may have things to impart that will help you. Liam, get some food and drink on the table.'

Clemens shook his head brusquely and his response was uncompromising. 'Not until I've seen to my horse's needs. I've pushed her hard today and doubtless will again. If you want a parley, follow me to the barn.' With that, he led the tired animal over towards that structure without inviting permission or even offering a backward glance.

His host was taken aback, but accepted the situation with good grace and a short while later he and his two sons joined Clemens in the barn. They had brought some beer, bread and cheese with them, which their guest began to dispatch with relish. Between mouthfuls he told them a little about himself.

'Obliged for the vittles, folks. My name's Clemens. John Clemens. My . . . our spread is up near Chinook.'

Even though preoccupied, he didn't miss the father's sharp intake of breath that greeted the disclosure of his name. That individual glanced meaningfully at his sons whilst considering a response. While he did so, Clemens took the time to examine each of them properly. All three were stocky, ruddy-faced fellows of average height. Liam, at roughly thirty years of age, was obviously the older brother to James. He possessed straw-coloured hair and fresh features. Observing the newcomer with wary interest, he was the first to speak.

'I reckon those are Sharps cartridges in your bandoliers,' he remarked. 'Would you be *the* John Clemens, buffalo hunter?'

Clemens momentarily stopped chewing. 'Sure don't know of another one with that name, although it's a while since I took a shot at one of those beasts. I pretty much worked myself out of a job.'

'So if you do catch up with those outlaws you could maybe pick them off at long range,' Liam persisted.

His father didn't like the way the conversation was going. 'Buffalo don't shoot back, son,' he added pointedly.

'But the redskins did,' Clemens chipped in sharply. 'And they didn't take kindly to their food source being slaughtered. Looking back on it all, I can kind of see their point of view, but it's too late now. The big shaggies are all gone and I consider that a shame.'

There was a brief silence, as the hunter seemed taken up by his recollection. Then Liam, who also seemed to have something on his mind, broke in on the reverie. 'When they left here, those fellas were heading towards the Missouri Breaks. Folks on the dodge usually hole up there for a while. If you're set on going in there after them, you'll need a guide. That'd be me!'

'Now just a god damn minute, Liam,' his father blurted out. 'I didn't raise you just to get shot to pieces by a bunch of saddle tramps.'

Liam smiled fondly at him, but there was no mistaking the determination on his face. 'It was my horse that they stole, Pa. And I'm of age an' then some, so you don't have any say in the matter.'

'But I do,' Clemens declared bluntly. 'Why should I want to hook up with someone I don't have the measure of?'

'Do you know your way around the Breaks?' the other man demanded.

'No. No, I don't,' Clemens admitted. 'But do you?'

'I know more about that part of the country than a jack rabbit knows about running,' Liam asserted confidently. 'Now in turn, you might know all there is to know about hunting men and critters, but if you go in there alone you'll surely end up as buzzard bait. The Breaks is not always as empty as you might think. It can attract some strange and dangerous people.'

Clemens stared at the younger man long and hard as he mulled over his options. In the course of his life on the frontier, self-reliance had generally seen him through, but he was pragmatic enough to know that there were times when that just wasn't enough. This was one of them.

'OK, I can work with that. *But*, you're after a horse and I'm after a wife, so I give the orders. Understand?'

Liam's eyes narrowed and he nodded grudgingly.

'So say it!' Clemens demanded harshly.

The young man twitched with surprise and glanced at his kinfolk. He obviously wasn't used to being spoken to in such a way, especially in his own barn, but then again he hadn't encountered the like of John Clemens before either. Finally and very reluctantly, he did as ordered.

'I understand.'

4

Lying flat out on top of the butte with the low sun off to his side meant that he could observe the new arrivals without any possibility of them spotting him. They rode along as though they owned the place, which made him smile a little because he had always considered the Breaks to be his domain. Then his craggy, bearded features froze with shock and he did a double take through the draw-tube spyglass. Tobacco juice trickled unnoticed over his matted chin, as his cycloptic vision crawled voyeuristically over every inch of the woman on horseback.

'Sweet Jesus, but she's a bonny lass,' he muttered in a still recognizable Scottish accent. For legal reasons relating to his notoriously vicious temperament, he had been gone from his isolated Highland haunts for upwards of twenty years, but his behaviour had not moderated in the slightest. After emigrating to America, he had quite naturally gravitated to another equally desolate spot, but he still retained his mother tongue.

He came to a decision there and then. Normally he would have kept clear of such a sizeable band of malefactors, but the presence of such a desirable female had changed everything. He couldn't exactly recall the last time that he had had a woman, but he did remember sourly that he'd had to pay for her. It had probably been around the time that he'd had his last hot bath down in Billings, but this time it was going to be different. This time there wouldn't be any money changing hands!

'I'm thinking you'll not be taking her away with you,' he confidently announced to the unsuspecting riders ahead of him, before crawling back to begin his precarious descent. From then on he would be their deadly shadow, unseen but perhaps not entirely undetected. Because for too long, he had preyed on unwary travellers and unimpeded success can make a man careless!

⋆ ⋆ ⋆

The scavengers had threaded their way through a varied selection of rock outcroppings until finally, just as the light began to drain out of the sky, they arrived at a small sheltered meadow on the northern bank of the Missouri River. Cottonwood trees lined the riverbank and it was an undeniably pleasant spot. At some point they would need to find a place to cross, but that could wait for another day.

'Get a fire going,' commanded Taw Johnson. 'And make it a big one. It's going to be a cold night.'

'For some more than others,' muttered Kenny Packard, as he sourly glanced over at Cathy. His left leg had finally healed up and he now had other things on his mind.

As was so often the case, Clay Bassett came up behind him unexpectedly. 'If he hears talk like that,' he murmured softly, 'he'll slit you from throat to crotch. And that might not be the only thing you have to worry about.'

Packard twisted around in alarm. 'Say what?'

Bassett groaned inwardly at the man's bovine expression. Good help really was hard to find.

'Call it a sixth sense or a gut feeling,' he elaborated, controlling his impatience. 'But I think we've had company ever since we entered the Breaks. Whoever it is is pretty damn good, but not up to some of the Indian trackers I've come across. If Taw didn't have other things on his mind, I reckon he too would have an itch he couldn't scratch.'

Packard's eyes widened in surprise. 'Do tell! So what do you want me to do?'

'Whoever's out there is most likely after the girl. I know I would be, if only to use her in trade. So tell the others to keep well clear of her, but otherwise to just act natural. That way she might draw them in. Once it gets full dark, I'll slip away from the fire to get my night vision and wait for something to occur.'

Packard nodded sagely, as though the whole idea had been his all along. 'You know what, Clay? You and I work real well together!'

Bassett's eyes glazed over slightly. 'I really can't recall what I ever did to deserve you.'

Taw Johnson spooned out a big helping of piping hot beans on to the bread on his tin plate. The freshly baked staple had come from New Haven and was a welcome addition. His guts rumbled with hunger, but unusually for him he also had someone else's welfare in mind. And so, after repeating the action, he lumbered over to join Cathy, a plate in either hand. The young woman looked up at him sourly, but made no comment as he settled himself next to her. Her hands were still bound.

'I'm going to take that rawhide off

you,' he said gruffly. 'Don't even think about running, 'cause there's nothing out there for miles except rough ground and wild animals. So even if the wolves didn't get you, you'd like as not break your neck in the dark.'

He unpicked the knots and she involuntarily groaned as the circulation was gradually restored to her hands. He chuckled and then began shovelling the beans into his mouth. Initially she tried to remain aloof, but the tempting aroma was just too much to bear. Her stomach was crying out for food and she was soon easily matching his crude eating habits. It wasn't until Cathy had wolfed it all down that she realized he was beaming broadly at her.

With a full belly, it felt natural to respond to his infectious grin, but just in time she recollected how she came to be there and so instead merely favoured him with a grimace. Taw shook his head in mock amazement and then snuggled a little bit closer.

'No point in looking so sour, little

lady. Some of them vittles came from your cabin.' He belched loudly, before restlessly shifting position in the grass. 'I had thought to steal a kiss from you and I think I still will, but first I've got business to attend to. Stay put!'

So saying, the outlaw leader clambered to his feet. Then, despite his pre-occupation, it suddenly occurred to him that something was amiss. He and the young woman were completely isolated on their side of the large fire. Since his men had no concept whatsoever of tact, there had to be another reason why they were all keeping clear. Then he began to feel another, stronger movement in his bowels and all suspicions were temporarily displaced by more base needs. Grunting, he swiftly moved off towards the river.

Clay Bassett lay flat out in the damp grass, some distance behind Cathy and well clear of the firelight. He was chilled to the bone and fighting back the desperate urge to move . . . something, anything just to generate some warmth.

The smell of food and the crackling of firewood were like torture to him, but some inner determination kept him in place. That son of a bitch Taw hadn't even noticed that his sidekick was absent, but Clay just knew that something was amiss.

He watched as the outlaw boss got to his feet and after a brief hesitation moved purposefully over towards the river. It was obvious what he was about and his departure meant that the girl was now completely isolated. If anything was going to happen, then it was likely to be soon. Bassett expectantly clutched his revolver, ready for the pounding of hoofs that would signify a lightning raid on the camp. And yet, as minutes passed, the only sounds came from his cronies as they stuffed their faces and basked in the warmth of the fire. Could it be that for once his sixth sense had entirely failed him?

His heart jolted with shock as a shadowy figure rose from the ground directly behind the girl. Surely no one could have got past him undetected? Numbed by the cold, Bassett could only watch as the wraith leapt forward and closed a foul-smelling hand over Cathy's mouth. Unable to cry out, she found herself dragged back, away from the welcoming ambit of the fire. The scavengers had not even noticed her sudden absence.

Unable to breathe and absolutely terrified, Cathy surrendered to panic and began to struggle violently. The sudden vicious blow to her head was stupefying and left her floundering, with all her muscle strength abruptly gone. After that, all she heard was the heavy breathing of her captor as he dragged her bodily away, much like a mountain lion might, to his lair. She was totally defenceless and lost to the world!

Then Clay Bassett, finally getting over his surprise, powered up from the ground and aimed his Colt Army at the kidnapper's broad back. Unfortunately, he had to cock it and the loud click resounded in the still night air. Twisting like the big cat with his prey, the intruder reacted to the totally unexpected challenge. With Cathy's body now in the way, Bassett had no choice but to hold fire, but not so his opponent.

The Scottish Highlander turned American outlaw instinctively aimed at the largest target, Bassett's torso. Accompanied by a bright powder flash from the muzzle, his revolver discharged its deadly load. The barrel must have dropped slightly, because the heavy bullet ripped into his victim's belly and that man dropped to his knees with an agonized howl. His companions around the far side of the campfire reached for their weapons in alarm, but with their night vision compromised, they merely milled around in confusion.

Taw Johnson had only just pulled his pants back up, but even so he reacted with remarkable speed. Intuitively realizing that the girl had to be involved, he grabbed his revolver and pounded back towards the camp, bellowing out, 'Hold fire unless you've got a target!'

The Highlander tightened his grip on his prize. He should really have finished his opponent, but he had been taken aback by that man's sudden appearance and with those in the camp stirring he needed to be gone ... quickly. Returning to the fore, he again dragged Cathy with him, but by doing so he lost her protective cover.

Despite the searing pain in his gut, Clay Bassett still gripped his Colt. He knew that he was in serious trouble, but nobody shot him and got away with it. Rapidly drawing a bead, he squeezed the trigger. The gun crashed out, but because he was on his knees the bullet went low, striking his enemy in the left thigh.

It was the kidnapper's turn to cry out. Suddenly his left leg just would not support him and he fell heavily to the ground. Despite the severe pain, he could still feel stunned disbelief at having been thwarted. Then Cathy tore away from his abruptly weakened grip and screamed out, 'Help me!'

With her frantic cry ringing in his ears, Johnson burst through his cordon of men and rapidly skirted the flames. Night fighting was not new to him and so he had kept one eye closed during the dash from the river. Peering into the gloom, he was now able to make out two figures apparently wrestling on the ground. Closing swiftly, he was soon able to distinguish Cathy's form and that of an unknown man. At the sound of the outlaw leader's approach, the hooded stranger twisted around and raised a revolver.

For such a big man, Johnson had fast reflexes. He aimed and fired in one smooth action. As the gun bucked in his hand, he shifted position and again squeezed the trigger. In quick succession, two bullets slammed into the Highlander's chest. The bludgeoning force smashed him back against the turf and all of a sudden he hadn't the strength left to squeeze anything. The revolver slipped from his fingers and with a last dying effort he glared up at his killer.

'Bloody Sassenach!' he hissed angrily and then fell back and was still.

Johnson was totally mystified by the startling turn of events. 'Who was that son of a bitch?' he barked. 'And what the hell is a Sassenach?'

Cathy was trembling with reaction. She reached her hands out for him to help her up and unthinkingly they tumbled into each other's arms. He protectively enveloped her shaking body and would have happily remained in that position had she not suddenly recollected just who he was. Shocked by her own behaviour, she struggled free, but not before the two of them had exchanged unexpectedly prolonged eye contact. Then she remembered Bassett and guilt overwhelmed her.

'Your friend took the first bullet,' she blurted out. 'He's over there.'

Startled, Johnson peered into the murk. He shivered involuntarily as he spotted his deputy. 'You men, follow me,' he yelled and soon fourteen men surrounded Bassett's pitiful figure. Still on his knees, he had fallen forward as though attempting to lessen the pain.

'Get him on a blanket and over to the fire,' Johnson commanded. 'We need to see how bad it is.'

As his men complied, the big man moved slowly and purposefully back to the body of their unknown assailant. His mind told him that Clay was finished, because nobody survived that kind of belly wound. His heart, however, prayed otherwise. They had ridden together for too long for it to end like this. As Cathy watched in horror, Johnson took careful aim at a set of bearded, lifeless features and grimly squeezed off a third shot. The bullet struck the Highlander between sightless eyes and would have made an effective *coup de grâce*.

Turning away from the gruesome corpse, he grimaced as a high-pitched scream resounded from over by the fire. The effort involved in moving Bassett had obviously severely tested him. Even so, Johnson did not immediately join his friend. Instead he remained motionless in the dark, carefully scrutinizing his surroundings as best he could. Just who else was out there? It was very unusual for a man to operate entirely alone, although of course the old time 'mountain men' had been known to. Finally, and very reluctantly, he headed back to the fire, reloading and holstering his weapon on the way. If others were stalking their camp, there was damn little that he could do about it until daylight and in the meantime there was a wounded man to attend to.

'Can't you give him some laudanum?' Cathy demanded on his return. In spite of her still being a prisoner, she knew that Bassett had very probably saved her from a much worse fate and his suffering touched her deeply.

Johnson shook his head regretfully. 'Trader Whiskey is all we have. Times haven't been easy lately.'

Bassett suddenly opened his eyes and

stared feverishly up at his boss. 'He's kilt me, Taw!'

'Like hell he has!' that man responded. 'Come daylight, we'll get that lead out of your belly and patch you up good as new.'

As Kenny Packard knelt next to the injured man and carefully poured some liquor into his mouth, Johnson suddenly recollected the earlier strange positioning of his men around the campfire. 'And what the hell were you lot doing, acting like my part of the fire had the plague? It certainly wasn't consideration and that's for truth.'

The outlaws regarded each other silently for a moment. It was a surly looking cuss named Vance who finally plucked up the courage to speak.

'Clay said we should keep clear of you, to maybe drew in that fella. Said you'd like as not would have smelt him yourself, only you was taken up with other things.' As he spoke, he glanced accusingly over at Cathy.

A volatile mixture of guilt and anger

flared up within Johnson's powerful frame. As colour flushed into his face, he squared his shoulders and took a step towards the suddenly very nervous scavenger. Then it dawned on him that he was the only person to blame for the situation. Drawing in a deep breath, he nodded regretfully.

'Then Clay got it right and I didn't, but I won't make that mistake again. I want a two man watch alternating throughout the night. Tomorrow we'll find out just who else is out there, because I don't believe one man alone would target a group our size.'

As the men drifted off, he glanced over at Cathy. She was trembling from a mixture of cold and reaction. Grabbing another bottle of whiskey and a blanket, he led her closer to the fire.

'Take a swig of this. It'll either perk you up or just maybe kill you,' he remarked ambiguously.

Against her better judgement she did so and was soon coughing and wheezing. 'What in God's name is in that stuff?' she finally managed.

'It's hard to tell,' he replied, with the makings of a smile. 'Like as not some chewing tobacco and red hot peppers have gone into it. It's no wonder it used to send the redskins on the warpath, but tell me you don't feel better and I'll call you a liar.'

Once she caught her breath, the young woman asked the question that was uppermost in her mind. 'What will happen to your friend? Will you leave him behind?'

Taw Johnson was genuinely shocked. 'Sweet Jesus, what kind of men do you take us for? We're outlaws, not animals! Come first light, we'll try and cut the bullet out. With or without that, he's like as not going to die, but one thing's for sure. Happen hell or high water, we're not moving from this place until he passes, because once you side with a man, you stick with him!'

5

The two men set off at first light. The morning was chilly and misty, but John Clemens had shown no hesitation in climbing out of his snug, hay-covered bedroll in the barn. For a very good reason, he was a driven man. He knew there would be no more nights under cover — unless he ended up in a cold hole in the ground — until he got what was left of his wife back. After hearing about the latest raid, such a grim mind set came naturally to him, because he was under no illusions that they were pursuing a band of very dangerous men. And such men would doubtless be relentlessly abusing Cathy's voluptuous body.

Liam's father and brother waved them off and then resolutely observed them until they were finally out of sight. Only then did the younger man turn to his silent travelling companion.

'So what do I call you? Clemens, John, sir or maybe even General, now that we are an army of two?'

'John has been my given name for forty-one years,' that man replied matter of factly. 'I reckon that'll serve well enough. *But* just remember that I'm the ramrod on this trip, so *don't* take liberties . . . otherwise I'll pound you into pulp!'

Liam regarded him askance. 'I don't see that there's any call for that attitude. We're in this together. I know you must be concerned about your wife, but . . . '

Clemens leaned sideways out of the saddle, so that his severe features crowded the other man's vision. 'You've no idea what I'm thinking on, sonny,' he snarled. 'In my time I've killed pretty much everything that's walked or crawled, so all I need from you is directions. Savvy?'

'Oh, I savvy,' Liam responded swiftly, so as to not give his odious companion time to repeat his demand. He decided that he'd obviously teamed up with a madman and he did just wonder how any woman could possibly tolerate him. She must be as ornery as he is, he decided.

★   ★   ★

Cathy gently patted Clay Bassett's florid forehead with a damp kerchief. Even though he was one of her kidnappers, she couldn't help but feel sorry for his terrible plight and yet his parlous condition did bring one compensation. Delirious and burning up with fever, he thankfully had little knowledge of the suffering that his body was enduring. One brief attempt had been made to extract the bullet, but that had soon been abandoned. It was lodged far too deep.

As she knelt by the fire next to her patient, she heard the sound of horses approaching the camp. Looking up, Cathy found Johnson's intense gaze on her. As their eyes met, he favoured her with a genuine smile before directing his attention to the single rider leading a spare horse that reined up before him.

'One set of tracks coming towards the camp and none going out, boss,' Jed reported. 'I found this mangy beast ground-tethered in those rocks over yonder. Looks to me like that cuss was on his lonesome.'

Taw Johnson regarded him intently. 'That's what you reckon, huh? But what if there's a pack of them out there and our man just fancied getting the jump on them to grab the girl first?' He toyed with the drawtube spyglass that he had taken from the body. 'They could be watching us through one of these right now and we'd be none the wiser.' The outlaw leader fell silent for a moment as he pondered his options, before finally nodding his head decisively.

'The Breaks obviously isn't as deserted as I thought and we're not going to be taken unawares again. Vance, take Davis and four others. You pick 'em. Strike off along the riverbank a couple of miles and then spread out and make a semicircular sweep around this camp until you hit the water again. Don't lose sight of each other and if you see *anybody*, send a rider hightailing it back here for me. Do *not* start shooting. Is that understood?'

'Yeah, yeah, I get it, Taw,' that outlaw responded. He had a powder burn on his cheek and a strange cast in one eye, which gave him a shifty demeanour that he had spent most of his life living down to. That characteristic suddenly became even more marked, as he uncomfortably shuffled his feet before speaking again. 'Thing is, boss,' he mumbled, 'a few of the boys were thinking that we should just move on out of here. Cross the river and carry on south before any more trouble hits us. After all, you might be right. There could be more of them.'

A chill settled over Taw Johnson's features that was evident to everybody watching. As he slowly scrutinized his men, a veil seemed to fall over his eyes that left the scavengers feeling uneasy without really understanding why. His right hand briefly brushed the butt of his Colt and then drifted away. Then, without any warning, he rapidly advanced on the unfortunate Vance. Seizing his throat in a vice-like grip, so that he instantly began to choke, Johnson addressed him in a tone that positively dripped with menace. It was obvious to everyone that his next words were meant for them all.

'Well, you can tell those boys that nobody who rides with me gets left behind until they've stopped breathing, which in your case might not be long. Anybody who can't work with that can leave now . . . but the next time I see them I'll kill them!' With that, he abruptly released his grip, allowing Vance to drop gasping to his knees.

'Now if you've stopped pissing around, I suggest you get on with what I told you. Oh, and heave that cadaver in the river. I'm sick of looking at it.'

As every man present eagerly nodded his assent, their fearsome leader turned away and looked over at Cathy Clemens. She had a strange look in her eyes, as though she was seeing the big man in a new light.

'Like I said last night,' he remarked softly. 'Outlaws, not animals!'

★　★　★

It was early afternoon when the terrain began to change. They left the ubiquitous Northern Plains grassland behind and entered a different world of steep bluffs and strange rocky outcroppings. The range at which a possible assailant could be spotted, dropped from miles to yards. John Clemens was suddenly out of his element and he knew it.

'Welcome to the Missouri Breaks, John,' Liam announced flamboyantly. It had not escaped his notice that his companion was looking distinctly uncomfortable with the change in surroundings. 'From now on, trouble could be around any bend and you wouldn't even know it.'

Clemens spat a stream of chewing tobacco from out of the corner of his mouth. The two men had been silent for hours, mainly due to his taciturn disposition, but he recognized that that would have to change. Yet it was also his nature not to compromise.

'If you want your horse back and a few others besides, you'll need me and this Sharps rifle, so don't get uppity.'

Liam regarded him calmly. 'Fair enough, but that works both ways. I've spent many weeks exploring and hunting round here. I know the trails, chokepoints and likely ambush sites. If those marauders are in the Breaks, I'll find them. Which means you *need* me to get your wife back. That kind of makes us partners, don't it?' With that, he favoured the older man with a knowing smile, which was almost guaranteed to annoy.

Deep down, Clemens recognized the logic in what he had just heard, but sadly the aggressive side to his personality just couldn't tolerate any level of disrespect from someone a good ten years his junior. He could feel his hackles begin to rise.

'Don't rile me, boy, or it'll go badly for you.'

That didn't sit well with Liam. Secure in his local knowledge, he no longer felt inclined to back down to an 'over the hill' buffalo hunter.

'You'd better walk softly around me, old man, or you'll wake up and find me gone.'

Clemens regarded him coldly for a moment and then leaned sideways in his saddle. 'Let me explain something to you,' he said mildly, before suddenly planting a right hook on the other man's jaw.

Things didn't work out quite the way Clemens had planned, however. Liam had anticipated the onset of violence and so was already rolling with the punch as it landed. Unable to stop his consequent slide out of the saddle, he was nevertheless able to inflict some damage on his way down. Kicking out with his left foot, he caught his opponent solidly under the chin and with a pained grunt, Clemens also tumbled out of his saddle.

Both men hit the ground hard at the same time. As their horses whinnied with fright and ran off, they desperately sucked air into their parched lungs. The younger man recovered first and scrambled to his feet. Racing towards his opponent, Liam again kicked out for a head-shot. Somehow, Clemens just regained his senses in time. Reaching out, he seized hold of the rapidly approaching boot and twisted with all of his strength. Abruptly losing his balance, his victim fell full length and was winded for the second time. Sensing the other man's vulnerability, Clemens got to his feet and leapt on top of him. Snarling with satisfaction, he landed first one and then a second haymaker on Liam's unprotected features.

★ ★ ★

Vance was the outermost rider of the cordon that advanced through the terrain surrounding their campfire. His nearest companion was only intermittently in view as they weaved through the broken landscape. The unkempt outlaw held little hope of actually flushing anyone out and so consequently was bored and inattentive. It was therefore with considerable astonishment that he suddenly came upon two strangers violently struggling on the ground. He abruptly reined in, his sluggish mind totally absorbed by the unexpected conflict. Unsurprisingly, they remained oblivious of his presence.

In Vance's considered opinion, the older man seemed to be getting the best of it, being both on top and dealing out some telling blows. But then a gloved thumb jabbed up into his eye and he howled out in pain and rolled away. Shaking his bloodied head, the younger man leapt up and launched yet another kick. This time it caught his victim in the ribs, causing him to reel backwards. Apparently sensing victory, he surged forward, only to have his feet neatly swept from under him by the older man's legs.

Now Vance had never been anywhere near the smartest of Taw Johnson's band and he was flummoxed as to how to react to the sight of the two men attempting to beat each other senseless. Somehow, to his way of thinking, their mutually destructive actions seemed to discount them as a threat. Then his boss's words came to mind. 'Do *not* start shooting.' Bemused by the whole business, he decided to return directly to the camp, collecting his companions on the way. So, gently tugging on the reins, he wheeled his horse away and went in search of the others.

As John Clemens clambered to his feet to renew the fight, some slight movement registered in his peripheral vision. Unlike the departing scavenger, he had no doubt whatsoever about his course of action. Drawing his Schofield, he cocked it and pointed it directly at his 'partner'.

'So you've brought a gun into a fistfight,' Liam remarked scathingly, as blood trickled from various cuts on his face.

'If I wanted to kill you, you'd already be dead,' responded Clemens impatiently. 'Now look over to your left aways and tell me we haven't just got lucky.'

Liam did as instructed and jerked with surprise. 'You think he saw us?'

'Of course he saw us. But I figure he didn't know what to do about us and he's reporting back. Get your horse and we'll follow him. That's if you've had enough of this childishness.'

'You started it,' the younger man replied grumpily.

Clemens gestured with his revolver. 'And I've just finished it. Now mount up!'

★　★　★

Taw Johnson regarded his minions incredulously, before focusing his rising anger on one individual. 'You dumb son of a bitch! You're telling me that you spotted two more strangers and you just plumb let them alone. Didn't it occur to you that they might be in cahoots with the mangy bastard who shot Clay? You know, the one that's feeding the fishes right now.'

Vance's misaligned eye began to twitch alarmingly as he realized his horrendous mistake and yet he tried hard to talk his way out.

'Aw hell, Taw. They was beating seven shades of shit out of each other. I reckoned it was just happenstance that brought them nearby. Didn't see no harm in it.'

Johnson kicked out savagely at a small stone, so that it flew past the other man's head like a musket ball. 'Well, it won't be happenstance that takes you back there, because I'm coming with you. And if your mistake costs us, you'll end up with both eyes at right angles, so help me God!'

The two pugilists had kept well back from Vance and his band, but it mattered not. They had the right direction and Clemens was beginning to get a feel for the situation. 'A big party will be secure in their numbers and likely camp right next to the river. You need to get us on to some high ground.'

Despite the pain in his head, Liam was beginning to realize that they were on to something. 'That butte over yonder will answer. It covers a good stretch of the water and all the land around. And we can get to it over some hard ground that'll hide our tracks.'

Even as they headed towards the impressive rock formation, there came the pounding of hoofs as a number of riders returned at speed to the scene of their brawl.

'Looks like somebody forgot something,' Clemens remarked drily.

★ ★ ★

Cathy gazed down on Clay Bassett's anguished, sweat-stained features and felt genuine sadness. The gut shot unfortunate's body was clearly enduring the tortures of the damned and there was not a blessed thing she could do about it, other than hold his hand and mop his brow. Mercifully, he remained oblivious to his own torment.

The remaining half a dozen or so scavengers regarded them both, when they could even be bothered to, with scant interest. As far as they were concerned, Bassett was already dead. They had also resigned themselves to the fact that Cathy was exclusively Johnson's girl, even if he hadn't, as yet, exercised his claim. Their leader's temporary absence allowed them to loll around drinking Trader Whiskey and smoking roll-ups.

It occurred to her that it would be relatively easy to grab a horse and skedaddle into the wilderness, but strangely she had no desperate urge to do so. She told herself that it was because she couldn't possibly abandon the pitiful wretch before her, but in truth it also had something to do with her growing interest in Taw Johnson. He hadn't turned out to be quite the brutal thug that she had expected. Then Cathy's face flushed with guilt as she recalled that she did still have a husband. The question was: would she ever see him again?

★　★　★

The two men couldn't possibly have known it, but they were occupying the exact same vantage point that the Highlander had used the day before. The butte was roughly some 700 yards or so from the scavengers' camp next to the Missouri River. The fact that it was situated at a forty-five degree angle from it also meant that they were perfectly positioned to observe the movements of the search party.

'Keep an eye on those fellas, while I see what we've got down there,' Clemens instructed. Extending his drawtube spyglass, he carefully scrutinized the encampment. Men lounging around the fire. Horses hobbled but not tethered, so as to allow them to drink from the river and forage. And then the sight that momentarily took his breath away. Cathy, apparently alive and well, kneeling in the grass.

He stared intently at her face, searching for cuts and bruises. The image quality of the old spyglass was not good, but she did not appear to have been superficially abused. Not that that covered his real concern. Then, as he noticed that she was tending to an injured man, unforeseen doubt began to creep into his mind. What was he to her and why were her hands not tied? There didn't even seem to be anyone watching her, so why didn't she make her escape?

Holding back the turmoil in his mind, Clemens moved his glass away from the camp and began to study its surroundings. Along with plenty of lush grass and wood for the fire, the outlaws had the river at their back, which was good defensively but could also work against them should they need to make a quick escape. Shifting his glass to the right, he then made a cursory inspection of the riverbank over to a point directly in front of his position. It was here that he received a second surprise.

Wedged between some rocks was the apparently dead body of a man. Clemens nodded pensively as he weighed up the possibilities. His discovery had to have some connection to the wounded man next to his wife. How he had ended up dead was irrelevant, but there was no doubt that a corpse could come in very useful.

'Those fellas are back where we had our set to,' Liam announced. 'Someone doesn't look right happy that we've gone.'

*   *   *

'What are we dealing with here, phantoms or shape shifters?' Johnson demanded sarcastically. 'Or maybe both men died and decomposed before we arrived.'

Vance stared around him dumbly, but then he had help from another of the gang. 'Blood spots down here, boss.' And then a few moments later, 'Tracks of two shod horses moving over to the rocky ground. We'd need an Indian to follow them any further.'

'Just great,' muttered the gang leader as he glowered at Vance. 'So we really don't know what we're up against yet.' He pondered for a moment. 'Right, back to camp. The light's starting to go, so there's no point stumbling around out here on the off chance. Just keep your eyes peeled.'

* * *

As they watched the group move cautiously back to the river, John Clemens began to reveal his plans to his astounded companion. 'Once they're back in camp, we're going after that stiff. And first off, I want his teeth!'

'Why in God's name would you want those?'

Clemens regarded him with genuine surprise. 'Because one way or another, I aim to turn a profit on this trip. Some dentists'll pay cash money for a good set of gnashers. Then again, with my luck, he'll probably have been a tobacco chewer. Anyway, what we're going to do then is . . .'

*　*　*

'How is he?' Johnson asked softly as he arrived next to Cathy and her patient. Instinctively, he already knew the answer. The blood-soaked bandages around Clay Bassett's midriff spoke volumes. As darkness began to fall, they both grasped that this could be his last night on earth.

'I've done all I can for him,' she answered wearily. 'Which isn't much under the circumstances.'

'I've seen such wounds before,' he

commented. 'Not even good doctoring would answer. All we can do is keep him warm and numbed with whiskey.'

As the fire was built back up to ward off the growing chill, the tempting aroma of food began to assail their nostrils. It was only then that the young woman realized just how hungry she was.

'I could eat a horse,' she announced.

Johnson favoured her with a broad smile. 'Let's hope it doesn't come to that.'

Taking Cathy by the arm, he gently helped her up and led her around the fire to where his men had a large pan of beans heating up. That simple action seemed so natural and yet its startling ramifications suddenly struck both of them at the same moment. It was as though they both knew that he was no longer her kidnapper and she was no longer his prisoner.

Gratefully she accepted a plate of bread and beans. Then, unbidden, she returned to Bassett's side. Beyond the light of the flames there was only inky blackness, but strangely it no longer held any fear for her. It was as if someone who had her interests at heart was now watching over her. Although Johnson remained with his men, their eyes kept meeting as though in some way they both knew that their relationship had changed.

After engaging in some ribald banter with his men and ensuring that the guards had been posted, he casually moved over to the far side of the fire. On the face of it he had come to check on his ailing friend, but Cathy was not fooled. It was quite obviously her company that he wanted and remarkably, she was able to acknowledge to herself that she welcomed his attentions. As the outlaw boss settled down next to her, Bassett cried out from the depths of his misery and she instinctively placed a comforting hand on the dying man's shoulder. By some quirk of fate, Johnson had the same idea and he suddenly found his meaty palm covering hers. She flinched slightly at his touch and then relaxed.

'What kind of a name is Taw anyway?' she suddenly demanded.

'My given name,' he responded hoarsely. 'And from now on it's what you call me. That is unless you want me to rope your hands together again.'

She shook her head firmly. 'I don't reckon you'll ever have cause to do that again.'

Any thoughts of rescue were now furthest from her mind, because she quite simply no longer considered herself to be a captive.

6

The two man hunters had passed most of the night at the base of the rock tower. With its solid bulk between their camp and the river, they had risked a small fire to heat some food and ward off the bitterly cold night air. Yet, even fed and moderately warm in their thick blankets, neither of them slept a great deal. Their thoughts were too full of what might occur the next day and when the first rays of light finally showed in the east, John Clemens gave no consideration to breakfast.

'It's time to make those thieving bastards bleed,' he announced grimly. 'Let's get aloft and make ready.' So saying, with his rifle slung over one shoulder, he began to ascend the steep face. The two heavy bandoliers clinked lightly against the rock outcroppings as he climbed.

For a long moment, Liam held back. Now that the time to shed blood had arrived and never having killed a man, he was suddenly nervous and unsure. Then the knowledge of how Clemens would view him struck home and he pulled himself together and followed on.

A short time later, the two men lay flat against the butte's cold, hard surface. The vigorous climb had stirred their blood and so Clemens deliberately proceeded slowly with his preparations. He had no intention of shooting until his breathing was completely steady. First, he used his spyglass to locate his wife's position in the riverside camp. That done, he set his Sharps down next to him and raised the rear ladder sight to make certain adjustments. The younger man was utterly astounded at the distance involved.

'Do you really think you can hit anything at that range?'

Clemens didn't even look up. 'I know I can and with the honest sights on this gun, I'll prove it. I'll grant you those sons of bitches are smaller than buffalo, but right now they're also not moving, which makes all the difference.' Thinking back to their laborious efforts of the night before, he couldn't resist a grim chuckle. 'And if things go to plan, when they do move they'll come closer to this beauty without even realizing it.'

Carefully removing a few cartridges from a bandolier, Clemens placed all but one of them within easy reach. Next he levered down the falling breechblock of his Sharps and slid the retained one inside. Then, tucking the butt tightly into his shoulder, he peered down the thirty-inch barrel towards the unsuspecting men that he was about to kill. The marksman was going about his preparations in such a single-minded fashion that his next remark took Liam completely by surprise.

'How come a young fella like you hasn't got a woman?'

The answer, when it came, was honest and sad in equal measure. 'Because the only women you get out on the frontier are either already married or whores and I don't fancy meddling with suchlike . . . although I'll grant you I've been sorely tempted on occasion.'

The older man grunted, quite obviously unimpressed. 'So jump a train back East and take your pick. It's what I did.' With that, he returned his full attention to the task in hand.

Picking out the first target was akin to playing God, because John Clemens had complete freedom of choice. The encampment was slowly coming to life, with one or two building up the fire and others preparing food. Seeking to cause maximum confusion, he decided to hit a lone individual who was standing upright nearest the fire. At such an immense distance, windage and elevation held great sway and therefore many considerations were going through the experienced hunter's head as he retracted the hammer. His finger tightened over the first of the double-set triggers and a man's life suddenly hung by a thread.

'I will see only the fire and those around it,' Clemens remarked. Liam, who was totally engrossed in the proceedings, again twitched with surprise, but listened intently as the sharpshooter continued. 'I'm relying on you to spot any of them making a break for it. If they should try to make it here on horseback, I will need to know about it.'

Then, without waiting for a reply, Clemens drew in a steady breath, held it and squeezed the second trigger. With a tremendous crash, the powerful rifle discharged its deadly load.

Kenny Packard had got as close to the rejuvenated fire as he could endure. The cold weather was making his recently healed thigh ache abominably and if there had been any laudanum in the camp, there would have been more than just Clay Bassett in line for it. As it was, he leaned forward slightly and attempted to massage some heat into his limb.

The bullet slammed into his back

and then, having flattened out, erupted from his chest in a great deluge of blood and tissue. The tremendous momentum tipped the traumatized man forward, so that he collapsed helplessly across the blazing fire. As sparks flew everywhere, the distant gunshot sounded off and Taw leapt up from his bedroll.

'What the hell just happened?' he demanded.

As Clemens smoothly lowered the Sharps under-lever, the empty brass cartridge flew out on to the rock in a little swirl of smoke.

'Pocket them all,' he instructed Liam, as he slid a fresh one into the breech. Then, as the block slid up into place, he minutely adjusted his aim. There was no noticeable urgency, but he was moving with practised speed. In his judgement, the element of surprise would only allow him one more shot and then things would get increasingly difficult. Cocking the hammer, he again squeezed the first trigger, then held his breath and fired. Even as his shoulder jerked under the recoil, the marksman instinctively knew that he had drawn a fine bead.

As Kenny's companions stared in shock at his twitching corpse, it was Taw who came to his senses first. 'Scatter and head for the trees,' he bellowed.

Before any of his men could react, a second projectile ripped into the small group preparing breakfast. This time a scrawny man with the improbable name of Scoot received the heavy bullet in his back. His bloody death was almost instantaneous, but unlike Kenny he wasn't destined for cremation.

If there had been any doubt that they were under attack, that second strike settled it. The *twelve* survivors abandoned everything and raced for the Cottonwood trees lining the riverbank. Unused to gunplay, Cathy merely stared after the retreating figures in horror, but unbeknown to the terrified young woman, Taw had deliberately excluded her. Whoever was out there, he knew full well that the last thing they wanted to do with a comely young woman was kill her.

As he took refuge behind a solid tree trunk, the outlaw leader yelled back to her, 'It's not you they're after. Just stay where you are.' Then, without awaiting her response, he transferred his attention to the terrain beyond her. 'Anybody see where that shooting came from?' he demanded of the others.

For long minutes there was total silence as his men desperately scrutinized the various bits of high ground. It was Vance, greatly eager to make amends for the previous day, who suddenly called out in triumph, 'I seen him, boss. Cockchafer's in amongst those boulders, directly ahead of us.'

Taw stared hard at the rocky ground on the edge of their meadow, some 300 yards away and sure enough there he was. A partially concealed figure holding a long gun was undoubtedly waiting for them to move back into the open.

Such was their mutual certainty that they had discovered their assailant that Taw didn't even bother to use the Highlander's spyglass for a closer look. He was also in no doubt as to what their next course of action had to be.

'We can't stay behind these trees 'til nightfall, 'cause he's bound to get lucky and pick some more of us off. So we're going to spread out and run full chisel for those rocks. If we fire as we move, it should keep his head down until we overwhelm the bastard. Any questions?'

A nervous voice piped up a few yards away, 'Well, yeah, what's overwhelm mean, boss?'

Not for the first time did Taw rub a meaty hand over his face in frustration. '*Jesus H. Christ*, why do I put up with . . . ?' The outlaw leader stopped abruptly as he realized that he had been unconsciously talking to his friend and deputy, Clay Bassett and a deep sadness came over him. 'It means, just shoot the bastard, savvy?' Again, without waiting for a response, he then called over to Cathy, 'Get flat to the deck and stay there. We're coming through!'

Taw waited until his men had drawn their weapons and then he gave the signal. In unison, they all leapt out from behind cover and raced pell-mell towards their enemy. Once past Cathy and Clay, they fired into the rocks. With their chests heaving from the unaccustomed exertion, accuracy was impossible, but the cumulative effect apparently served to prevent any return fire. Even though his legs were leaden and his lungs parched, Taw felt a surge of exhilaration as they drew nearer. They were actually going to make it!

★   ★   ★

'Oh my, will you look at that?' cried Liam as he stared down at the rousing sight. 'Those silly bastards think it's Gettysburg all over again.'

His companion had to admit that their ruse was working well, but he had something else on his mind. 'Why the hell doesn't she make a break for it? There's horses a-plenty and no guards.' John Clemens wanted to scream out to her, but had to settle for merely shaking his head in disbelief. 'We'll be having words when this is all over,' he added ominously.

'Never mind that,' hissed Liam urgently. 'You've got some more targets down there.'

Nodding his acknowledgement, the deadly sharpshooter slightly altered position to his left and emptied his mind of everything other than the task at hand. After a minor adjustment of the ladder sight to compensate for the reduced range, he was ready.

Unused to life out of the saddle, the twelve men were almost dead on their feet, but quite remarkably they had covered the distance without having once been shot at. As they closed in from all sides, Taw bellowed out, 'Blast him,' and they did. A dozen revolvers repeatedly spat bullets and for a moment or so a dense cloud of powder smoke obscured their front. Then it cleared and they all whooped for joy. Their unknown foe had been thrown back by the sheer weight of lead and could no longer harm them.

'That's him paroled to Jesus,' Vance crowed happily.

'Yeah, we sure dished him,' Jed agreed, as he clambered over the intervening boulder.

Then Taw swore bitterly and they all froze with shock. The same corpse that he had gratuitously blessed with a headshot, prior to it being hurled into the freezing cold Missouri River, had returned to haunt them all. Punctured with fresh bullet holes, it now possessed skin that had turned waxy grey and a peculiarly macabre grimace that was emphasized by a complete lack of teeth. Its 'rifle' turned out to be a tree branch trimmed to size.

'By Christ, we've been stalking a dead man. Someone's going to answer for this,' Taw vowed angrily.

The man next to him abruptly jerked forward and coughed blood. Even as a distant gunshot rang out, the latest victim helplessly dropped to his knees. Taw momentarily steadied him, so as to check on the entry wound. With the trajectory direction confirmed, he reluctantly allowed the man to fall to the ground and yelled out, 'We've been suckered. Get round here behind these rocks.'

As all *eleven* men did so, their leader simultaneously withdrew his spyglass from a pocket in his buckskin jacket. He was fleetingly distracted by the sight, directly before him, of their comrade twitching in his death throes. With an effort of will, Taw dragged his gaze away and wedged the glass in a crack between two rocks. Desperately, he began to scan the nearest high ground for any signs of movement. He continued with this for a few minutes, during which there were no further shots.

'Where the hell is he, Taw?' whined one of the men impatiently. 'He can't be a ghost.'

Ignoring him, that man gradually extended his search further out until finally he happened upon a tower like butte about 600 yards away. Panning up the side of it, he suddenly recoiled with astonishment at the sight of a rifle muzzle seemingly aimed directly at him. Ducking down, he exclaimed. 'Damn, but he's good!'

Myriad thoughts passed through the outlaw's mind as he anxiously tried to weigh up their limited options. One thing was for sure: superior numbers counted for nothing in their situation. At length, he came to a decision and it was not one that he relished.

'Our shooter's atop that butte, over yonder,' he improbably announced, Ignoring their cries of disbelief, he remorselessly carried on with, 'I glimpsed one other man with him, which would tie in with what Vance said yesterday. Only now they're not fighting each other anymore. They're after us. And at such a distance we've no chance of hunting them down without our horses, so we'll have to leg it back to camp. With just these belt guns, we can't even attempt covering fire. It's every man for himself, boys.'

As his men huddled miserably behind their rocks, they recognized that there really was no other choice. Jed, mean-looking at the best of times, spoke for them all when he stated, 'All this running and hiding shit don't sit well with me, Taw. There'd better be some pay back.'

'There will be,' their leader agreed. 'But for now, let's just get the hell out of here. On my command. Three, two, one, go!'

As they again leapt from cover, every single man knew that there was a reloaded rifle aimed at someone in the scattered group. But as in time of war, each of them prayed that the bullet would have another name on it. As Jed lurched into action, the unaccustomed exercise painfully jarred his ankles, but it was nothing to the searing agony that suddenly engulfed his right thigh. Accompanied by the distant gunshot, blood welled up through the rent in his trousers leg and the scavenger uncontrollably tumbled to earth.

Out of all the frantically running men, Taw was the only one to stop. Even as he viewed Jed's distress, the reason for the none-lethal wound instinctively dawned on him. The hidden assassin was testing their courage and resolve by intentionally burdening them with another wounded man. Even whilst acknowledging the cunning in such a plan, rage began to build within him. He and his men were being treated like rats in a trap!

Steeling himself for what he knew had to be done, Taw slowly and deliberately walked over to the stricken outlaw and aimed his revolver at the horrified individual. Then, for what seemed like an age, he just stood there ignoring Jed's pitiful cries and gazed over at the butte's occupants. It was almost as though he was inviting death. Daring the bastard to shoot him, whilst at the same time hinting that he might well finish off his own man in cold blood. Taw was playing a dicey hand, but in the heat of the moment he just didn't give a damn.

★　★　★

'Why the hell don't you pop a cap on him?'

Clemens's eyes never left the audacious, buckskin clad figure as he replied, 'He's a very brave man, but that's not a good enough reason to let him live. No sirree. But he's got me curious as to what he'll do and because of that I'm thinking he must be their leader. And if he's what's keeping Cathy in one piece, it might be better to let him live . . . for a while. Until I've whittled his men down a bit more.' His strangely cold eyes suddenly settled on Liam's. 'Don't you think?'

His companion shrugged uncomfortably. There was a chillingly cold-blooded aspect to the man hunter that was beginning to make him nervous. The excitement

111

of the chase was definitely losing its attraction.

'If you say so,' he reluctantly managed. 'But I thought we were here to get your wife and my horse back. Not murder all those men in cold blood.'

Clemens slowly eased the hammer down and then glanced back at the audacious outlaw. He nodded thoughtfully, as the big man heaved his wounded companion on to his shoulders and staggered off towards the river.

'They shouldn't have taken what was mine. Did you know that I once killed over a hundred buffalo in one day? If the skinners could have kept pace with me, I'd have slaughtered way more. Those dumb creatures just stood there and dropped, one by one. Kind of like those fellas are doing!'

7

Despite the chill air, sweat was pouring from Taw by the time he got back to the river. As he thankfully lowered Jed to the ground, he was aware that some of his men were regarding him sheepishly. Not one of them had turned back to help him and that only served to fuel the anger that was burning inside.

'Looks to me like his leg's broke. Cut some splints and see to him. You can do that, can't you?'

Two of them scurried off to comply and were glad to do it. Their leader was a fearsome sight when his blood was up. A man called Davis finally plucked up the courage to ask the question that was on everyone's lips.

'What we gonna do now, boss? We can't just hide in these trees forever, like god damn squirrels.'

Taw squinted at him fiercely. 'No.

No, we can't. But so long as that cockchafer sits up on the butte with his festering buffalo gun we can't attack him, either. On foot we'd be too slow and on horseback we'd make too big a target.'

A soft voice behind him brought him up short. Remarkably, he had completely forgotten about Cathy.

'I heard you say buffalo gun. My husband has a Sharps rifle. He used to be a buffalo hunter. I think that's how he earned the money to buy our place.'

The big man's eyes widened. 'Tell me his name again.'

'John Clemens,' she hesitantly replied. 'Some folks in Chinook told me he used to be famous.'

The outlaw boss stared at her incredulously, even more colour flooding into his already flushed features. 'Sweet Jesus. With shooting like that it must be him. And who's he likely to have with him? For sure he's not alone and then there was that other freak that we threw in the river.'

The young woman shrugged nervously. 'John kept pretty much to himself. He isn't too good with people. Maybe it's someone else you've upset.'

Despite the parlous situation, Taw erupted into laughter. 'Well, that don't narrow the field much. We've upset folks in nearly every state and territory of the Union.'

Before she could comment, there came a tremendous whinnying from over by the horses, followed by a distant and all too familiar gunshot. As everyone turned to watch, one of the animals keeled over, blood pouring from its belly.

'Well, that's no surprise. He's after the horses now,' the outlaw boss remarked with bleak acceptance. 'Round 'em up, boys, pronto. If we're left afoot out here, we're finished.'

Nobody needed any urging. A horse, saddle and firearms were all most of them had in the world. Desperately they raced over to the nervous animals, but even as they did so, another high-powered cartridge discharged on the butte. The agonizing death of a second horse enraged the scavengers. Some of them had had the wit to grab their repeating rifles and they now halted and loosed off a hail of lead at their tormenter. A dense cloud of sulphurous smoke was soon drifting over the meadow, but that was all that their wild shooting achieved.

'Save your powder,' Taw bellowed. 'There's nothing we've got that has the range.'

Cursing impotently, his men untied the hobbles and leapt on to the surviving animals. Another shot resounded over the Breaks, but a combination of movement and smoke mercifully ensured that it went wide. Digging heels into their horses' flanks, the men charged back to the temporary safety of the Cottonwoods. Behind cover again, a couple of hotheads renewed their pointless shooting, until Taw offered them better advice.

'If you've just got to pop some caps, use them on those poor creatures and put them out of their misery,' he ordered, pointing at the two wounded beasts. Then, as his men complied, he turned towards Cathy. 'How's Clay?'

'Still clinging to life,' she replied. 'He must have tremendous willpower.'

'Maybe,' Taw allowed. 'Or maybe he's just terrified of dying like the rest of us. Either way, we can't tend to him over there. We have to get him back into the trees.'

'Use me,' she replied without hesitation. 'If I stay between you and John, he won't risk a shot. And after watching you bring that man back, I don't think you're scared of any living thing.'

The big outlaw regarded her curiously. 'Just what's occurring here? Why would you want to help us? That murdering son of a bitch is your husband, remember? He's here to rescue you.'

Even though very conscious of the many eyes suddenly on her, Cathy seemingly took an age to reply. What she finally said stunned Taw and those others straining to hear. 'Perhaps I'm just not ready to be rescued . . . yet. I don't know. When you took me from my home, I wanted to hurt you, but now . . . Well, what John is doing just doesn't seem right. He's deliberately making you and your men suffer. I guess I'm seeing a nasty streak in him that doesn't sit well with me.'

Taw shook his head in amazement. 'Jeez! You really are full of surprises, lady. I thought you'd be jumping for joy at all this bloodshed on your behalf.'

'Maybe that's because you don't know me very well.'

Taw's brow furrowed deeply as he edged closer. He felt slightly breathless at the apparent possibilities in her remark. 'I can't think of anything more I'd like to do,' he quietly replied. 'But right now we need to get over to Clay. And seems to me it might look better if you were under my gun. Savvy?'

She nodded her understanding as they stood up together. Drawing his revolver, he gently wrapped his left arm around her neck and placed the muzzle against her right temple.

'No shooting,' he sternly informed his men. 'I don't want to provoke that bastard into chancing a shot. The fact that he missed with his last one at least proves that he's human like the rest of us.'

Very slowly, the two of them emerged from the trees. They stood for a moment to allow Clemens to size up the situation and both of them felt the sudden tension brought on by their total vulnerability. Then, at Taw's command, they moved steadily towards the fire. He was very conscious of her body pressing against his, but that pleasurable sensation swiftly departed as they closed in.

Kenny's dreadfully charred body lay next to the dying flames. Cathy had managed to drag it out of the fire, but not before his features had been terribly disfigured. Unbelievably, Clay Bassett was still alive and Taw was in no doubt about what needed to be done.

'This is going to hurt him, but there can be no help for that. I'm going to get him under his armpits and drag him back. That way I can point my gun at you and still keep you between me and that butte.'

Bracing himself against both the effort and Clay's reaction, Taw allowed her to move away from him. Reaching down, he took a firm hold and heaved. Every man in the trees heard the resulting scream.

★ ★ ★

John Clemens stared fixedly through his spyglass. He had to admit that the big outlaw had brains as well as grit. He had ensured that Cathy remained between the sharp-shooter and his target at all times. And yet, as before, Clemens harboured a vague suspicion that things were not all they seemed. His wife displayed no visible restraints and she had had ample opportunity to leap on a horse and hightail it out of there.

'I think we've been up here long enough,' his companion suddenly announced.

'Sooner or later those lowlifes are going to surround this lump of rock. If nothing else, they could seize our horses and starve us out.'

'*You think we've been up here long enough,*' Clemens mimicked scornfully.

'What would a Montana settler know about long range man killing? I'll tell you what we're gonna do. We're going to stay right where we are until nearly dark and then *we'll* close the distance. They can't go anywhere in daylight with two wounded men and in the meantime, I might just be able to pick off something else.'

★ ★ ★

It was the persistent scavenger Davis who finally said what most of his cronies were thinking. 'This young filly might be real purdy, but she ain't worth dying for. I say we put her on a horse and send her back to that scum-sucking husband of hers. Then, just maybe, he'll stop blowing holes in us.'

Taw regarded him balefully for a moment. 'Is that so? And what if getting her back ain't enough for him? What if he's out for revenge no matter what and happens to have a taste for killing? Where would we be then without this young *filly*? With no hostage and us as buzzard bait, that's where! And besides, we got three dead and two wounded by that cuss. Seems to me we're due a reckoning.' He paused a moment to let that sink in, before demonstrating that he had been doing some thinking of his own. 'So this is what's going to happen. I want two travois built and ready for nightfall. Once it drops dark, everything changes and that god damned Sharps counts for doodly squat. Some of you will head south through the Breaks with the wounded. Those that want some pay back can stay with me.'

He sensed rather than saw Cathy flinch next to him and lowered his voice. 'You and me will have to talk. You've got a big decision to make before dusk. Because, one way or another, that John Clemens is going to bleed!'

Things were moving too quickly for Davis. 'Just how the hell are we supposed to get two wounded men across that river? That's why it's called the *Missouri* Breaks, 'cause the Missouri runs through it,' he added sarcastically.

'You build the travois and I'll show you why I'm still the boss of this outfit,' replied Taw sharply.

By the time the last vestiges of light began to drain out of the sky, everything was prepared. Even the ornery Davis had to admit that the plan was good. An acceptable crossing point, partially tested by Taw behind a screen of trees, had been located one hundred yards down river and was therefore further away from the butte. Two travois had been constructed out of off cuts from the Cottonwoods, to transport the injured men Indian fashion. With long parallel poles stabilized by a third and then bound together by rawhide and a network of small branches, the conveyances could be dragged along behind the horses. Taw was well aware that the two men would suffer terribly from the jarring movement, but there was simply no help for it.

For the initial crossing, Jed had agreed to grit his teeth and ride over on horseback. Clay's travois had been strapped across the backs of two spare horses that were to be led to the south bank: an arrangement that would hopefully keep him above the water level. With the time to move almost upon the depleted band of scavengers, it was decision time for Cathy. Taw took her to one side and placed his hands gently on her shoulders.

'We're all going across that river. Then the main group are heading south, while I remain near the riverbank with a couple of the boys. I aim to finish Clemens, along with whoever else is with him. You've no say in that, but I will give you a choice. You can either go with my men or take off by yourself once you're clear of the area. I guess I owe you that much.' He paused to give her time to take that in before asking, 'So which'll it be?'

Her lovely eyes widened at the stark options. 'So after all this, you're just turning me loose?'

For the first time since New Haven, his features registered embarrassment. 'I never foresaw any of this. The killings and more especially you. I guess lust has become something more. All I know is that I don't want to see you hurt.'

'And yet you intend to kill my husband!'

The more customary determination returned to his face. 'Violence is our trade, lady. You've got to understand that. I never expected to meet someone like you out here, but that can't change what's going to happen to John Clemens. He drew first blood, so I've got to end it!'

'Boss!' Davis hissed. 'We need to go.'

Taw stabbed a finger directly at him. 'One minute,' he snarled, before returning his full attention to Cathy. 'Decide!'

Despite the cold, she could feel her palms growing clammy. Her heart was beating furiously. Out of all the homesteads in Montana, why had this man picked hers to raid? The words suddenly came in a rush. 'I'll stay with your men. At least until you catch up. But I really don't know how it's come to this.'

His relief was obvious and touching. A broad smile spread across his face. Both of them understood the full import of what she had just said. On impulse, his right hand briefly reached out for hers. 'It must be my roguish charm,' he quietly responded. Then, turning to his men, he barked, 'Let's ride!'

★ ★ ★

The two men timed their descent to coincide with the fall of darkness. Liam had held his peace throughout the awkward climb, but as they finally mounted their horses, he could restrain himself no longer. 'Riding over to their camp seems kind of reckless to me.'

John Clemens grunted scornfully. 'Why so? They'll all be gone by the time we get there.'

The younger man couldn't hide his surprise. 'Didn't reckon on that big fella leaving his wounded behind.'

'Hunting critters teaches you a lot. After watching him earlier, I know he won't have,' Clemens responded with absolute certainty. 'But they'll be gone all the same. They took a beating this morning that they won't care to repeat. Now enough talk. You just concentrate on leading us to the river and then I'll take over.'

Even though he complied, Liam regarded the other man with belligerent silence. He was getting mighty tired of playing second fiddle to a 'blowhard'. So much so that he actually contemplated cutting loose from his dominating companion.

Only after much thought did he finally decide to see what the night brought, before doing anything drastic.

★ ★ ★

Jed cried out in pain as his wounded leg jarred against the saddle. It served to compound his misery of being immersed up to his waist in freezing water. He had elected to stay off the travois until they reached the other side, but was definitely regretting it.

'Hush up, you noisy bastard!' Davis called over. 'You'll give us away to that tarnal buffalo hunter.'

Taw, coming up the rear, gave him short shrift. 'Back up, Davis. That son of a bitch already knows what we're about and I want him to come after us.'

As the fugitives made their way across the Missouri, Bassett began to mumble insensibly. Atop the two roped travois, he was above the water level, but the pitching and jawing movements of the two tethered animals unsettled him. Such an attempt would have been impossible after a spring thaw, but even so the horses made heavy going of it.

Cathy had more on her mind than the numbing cold. Even as they approached the inky blackness of the south bank, she kept nervously glancing behind her. Somewhere back there was a husband with murder on his mind and such a thought gave her no comfort whatsoever.

* * *

'They've gone,' whispered Liam, as the two men cautiously advanced through the trees. The surprise in his voice was very evident and gave Clemens cause to smile inwardly.

'Hmm, tell me something I don't know,' he retorted. 'Question is, are they *all* hot-footing it south, or is there a welcoming committee on the other bank?' Clemens took a moment before making up his mind. It never even occurred to him to consult with his companion. 'Follow me,' he commanded.

★ ★ ★

All of his able-bodied men had elected to remain behind with Taw, but he had deliberately restricted the numbers. Two would be enough, because he didn't want them tripping over each other in the gloom. He also knew that their pursuers were unlikely to use the same crossing point and from past experience he was able to recall the location of the only other one within a reasonable distance. As a consequence, the three outlaws were spread out behind some rocks directly opposite that spot, but well back from the river. Their mounts were tethered out of hearing range.

'Nobody shoots until I do,' he commanded, as he levered up a cartridge from the Winchester's tubular magazine. The full dark of a cloudy night was upon them, but it would still be possible to make out the moving shapes of men and animals against the flow of the Missouri.

'All the tracks go into the river here, so you need to take us across elsewhere,' remarked Clemens softly.

'Well, I just *happen* to know of another place only a spit from here. So stay close old man, 'cause I'm not coming back for you if you should wander off and get lost,' Liam replied with quiet satisfaction and set off carefully along the riverbank.

'Question is, do *they*?' Clemens said to himself, concealing his anger as he followed on.

The screen of trees that had served the outlaws so well was now on their left. After a short distance, Liam urged his horse over to the water's edge.

'This is it,' he whispered.

Clemens drew his Schofield. A single shot Sharps had no place in any night fight. 'You know the lie of the land,' he replied equally quietly. 'I'll follow you across.'

Liam glanced at him sharply. He had

a vague suspicion that he was being manipulated, but it was no time to be arguing. As the two riders entered the seemingly impenetrable dark waters, a freezing chill took their breath away. Ahead of them, on the far side, lay more broken ground and what should have been a comforting silence.

In the dead of night, any metallic movements would sound like an anvil strike, so the waiting scavengers already had their weapons cocked and ready. Taw watched as the dark shapes came up out of the river and the hairs on the back of his neck tingled. He had second-guessed their assailants and now it was pay back time. Taking careful aim at the first horseman, he began to contract his forefinger. Confident that his own men would not preempt him, he waited a full minute as the two riders drew nearer. A grin of pure savage delight creased his features as he finally closed his eyes and fired.

8

By intentionally avoiding the blinding muzzle flash, Taw failed to witness its direct result, but he was in no doubt of the outcome. Rapidly working the under-lever, he pumped up another cartridge and then rolled sideways. Only then did his eyes snap open, to be immediately dazzled by a flash from an opposing weapon.

As Taw's shot rang out, John Clemens reacted with almost animal speed. Even as his companion slumped under the impact of a bullet, he fired once for effect and then flung himself sideways out of the saddle. Two shots crashed out simultaneously from in amongst the rocks and although they had given their positions away, neither of the men obeyed the 'fire and move' rule. Conversely, Clemens had barely hit the ground, before he was in rapid motion. Powering to his feet, he raced around the side of his opponents. They suddenly had a deadly foe on their flank, but with their night vision temporarily lost, they didn't even know it.

As the first gunshot crashed out behind her, the jarring shock literally caused Cathy to jump in her saddle. With other discharges following on, her terrible anxiety only increased. Men were likely dying back by the riverbank and for some wholly illogical reason, it was Taw Johnson's survival that concerned her most. On sheer impulse, she tugged the reins around and urged her horse back towards the firefight. One of the scavengers yelled out something unintelligible, but she completely ignored him and was quickly swallowed up by the murk. More gunshots rattled out in rapid succession, serving to increase her fears, but leaving little doubt over the direction to follow.

Hearing movement, Johnson's two men simultaneously realized their dreadful error, but by then it was too late.

Initially keeping one eye closed, Clemens emptied his revolver into them with lethal efficiency. First a shot in the chest for the nearest, then, as that man staggered sideways, two more into his partner, bringing that man to his knees. Next, having opened his other eye, he moved round behind them and favoured them both with a single headshot. Well aware that his weapon was empty, the skilled shootist made another change of direction and then backed away. Breaking the Schofield open, he ejected the empty cartridges on the move. He only just avoided disaster, as the Winchester that had settled Liam crashed out a short distance away. Feeling the blast of pressure from the bullet, he dropped to his knees and swiftly reloaded his revolver by feel alone.

Even to a man skilled in gunplay, there was something chilling about the professional efficiency of the shooting. The resulting silence convinced Taw that his men had to be stone dead. This son of a bitch Clemens had obviously killed far more than just dumb animals in his time. He knew when to move and how to shoot, both at extreme range and up close. If the outlaw boss was ever going to finish him, then it had to be there and then, before he reloaded. Because if the assassin did get away, they'd soon all be at the mercy of that damned Sharps again.

Taw aimed slightly to the right of the last muzzle flash, fired and immediately shifted position, working the lever-action as he did so. Then, with the Winchester's butt tucked tightly into his shoulder, he waited in silence for some kind of movement.

Anything that might give him the edge that he so desperately needed. The pounding of shod hoofs off to his right took him completely by surprise. Surely there couldn't be another accomplice?

Cathy had never felt so desperately uncertain. She couldn't see another living thing and yet somehow she could feel the presence of others. Then her heart leapt, as a hand seemed to literally come from nowhere and grabbed her bridle.

'What in tarnation are you doing here?' Taw hissed angrily.

'Looking for you, of course,' she responded, with a mixture of relief and concern. 'I heard shots. I thought maybe . . . '

Taw shook his head with dismay. His priorities had abruptly altered. John Clemens would have to wait. Instead, since a bullet in the dark was no respector of persons, he had to get the girl to safety. Somehow, it never occurred to him to announce her arrival to their deadly shadow, because remarkably the lovely young woman had already stated that she had come for him and not her husband!

With his 'cavalry' sidearm reloaded, Clemens listened intently for any movement. He got more than he bargained for when he heard what he could only assume was a horse *man* unexpectedly approaching. Since it had to be one of the outlaws returning to help his leader, he dropped flat to the ground to wait on events. Would they, with yet two more dead men, merely break off the action and escape, or instead try to run him to earth in the dark?

The sound of two horses moving off provided his answer and in spite of the situation he laughed out loud. They had passed up on their best chance of killing him, because from then on he would only ever strike from long range.

An anguished cry drifted over from near the river and he suddenly recalled his unfortunate companion. A lot of help he turned out to be, he considered grimly *and* unfairly.

After cautiously waiting for a few moments, he first confirmed that both his victims were in fact dead and then slowly made his way back to the riverbank. In one of his pockets were the few meagre coins that he had taken from the cadavers. Vengeance was one thing, but he still expected to get a return on the cost of his cartridges.

Their horses had not strayed far in

the darkness and on inspection, he found with relief that his 'truthful' Sharps was still in its scabbard. Only then did he check on Liam's condition. For a man well used to death, it was immediately apparent that the young man was in a bad way. Blood foamed from his mouth and glistened over his jacket. His remaining time on God's creation was limited and unfortunately John Clemens was not the man to make it any easier for him.

'Is that you, Pa?' the dying man suddenly called out.

Clemens grunted. 'I ain't your pa and I don't reckon you'll be seeing him again any time soon.'

The harsh unfeeling tone brought Liam back to temporary lucidity. He seemed to sense that he was to be abandoned to his fate.

'For pity's sake, don't leave me all alone!' he pleaded.

The man hunter gazed down at him with a total lack of compassion. 'You're shit out of luck, fella. I've got a trail to follow and that don't allow any time for doctoring.' With that, he grabbed the dying man's belt gun and tossed it out of reach. He had no intention of being shot in the back as he departed.

Some inner reserve of strength prevented Liam from pleading anymore, but he did have something to say. 'I hope your woman gets taken clear down to Mexico, you miserable bastard. They can't be any worse than you below the border.'

★ ★ ★

First light found the ten remaining scavengers and their former prisoner still threading their way through the badlands on their relentless way south. Although their progress was painfully slow, Taw had insisted that they keep moving throughout the night. They had rested up for much of the previous day and he was instinctively certain that Cathy's husband had survived and would be on their back trail. She, in turn, was uncomfortably aware that by returning to search for her former captor, she had very probably prolonged their deadly ordeal. And yet, it was that very realization that crystallized her new situation in her mind, because she now very definitely considered John Clemens to be the enemy and not Taw Johnson. How that was going to affect her future was still just too much to take in.

'It's not your fault,' the latter individual suddenly remarked. 'I brought all this on by kidnapping you in the first place.'

Startled by his prescience, she turned wide-eyed towards him and instinctively favoured the big bluff outlaw with a warm smile. Immediately behind them, a young man named Curtis observed the mutual affection with undisguised envy. He sorely wanted a young woman of his own, if only to brag to his cronies, but alas, it was never going to happen. With outstanding accuracy, the heavy calibre bullet struck his unwashed skull, causing it to explode like a ripe melon. As the ghastly corpse toppled sideways, the fugitives heard the frighteningly familiar reports of a Sharps rifle come to them from the north.

Even as Cathy screamed at the horrific sight, Taw bellowed out, 'We've got to ride like the wind. Once we reach open country that bastard'll lose some of his edge. Keep the spare animals behind us to throw his aim.'

Jed, already in great pain from his leg, rolled off his travois and hobbled to the nearest horse. 'I'll take my chances in the saddle, boss, but if we drag those things at speed it'll likely finish Clay.'

Taw glanced down at his friend strapped tightly to the conveyance and for a moment his eyes grew moist. Then the reluctantly hardened his heart and retorted, 'Well then, so be it. We've done all we can for him and more. Now move out!'

The nine riders dug their heels in hard and they were off. With the spare horses running at the rear and all the dust raised by the bucking and twisting travois, there was little chance of any more casualties . . . except for the amazingly resilient Clay Bassett. As the tremendous pounding reached his brave heart, it finally gave out. Sadly it was to be some time before anyone noticed, because they were all distracted by Jed's anguished cries and the effort involved in avoiding rocks and gopher holes and such.

To the desperate marauders, who weren't used to such sustained flight, it seemed an age before their leader finally eased the pace. Ahead of them was open grassland, which signified at long last that they were clear of the Breaks, with all of its god damned buttes and cliffs that they had initially so welcomed.

'Once we're out in that sea of grass, there'll be nowhere for him to hide,' Taw announced, with a show of confidence. 'He'll have to keep back . . . hopefully even out of his range.'

He turned to inspect his depleted band and only then did he notice

Bassett's lifeless body, lolling limply on the travois. For the second time that day, tears welled up in his eyes.

'Oh, hell!' he mumbled sorrowfully. Dismounting, he wandered over and stared down at his friend for what seemed to the others like a dangerously long time.

'We're going to bury him,' he abruptly proclaimed.

Vance's suspect eye and vivid powder burn suddenly seemed to endow him with a sinister quality, as he glowered over at his leader. 'That don't seem right sensible, boss. We need to keep moving, what with that son of a bitch on our tail an' all.'

Taw drew in a shuddering breath and turned to face a very nervous outlaw. 'That man and I have ridden together for over a decade,' he growled thunderously. 'He was a good friend to me and in case you don't recall, he looked out for some of you fellows as well. I didn't abandon him in the Breaks and I ain't leaving him to rot here now he's dead. I don't care if the devil himself is on our tail. Now all of you get digging. The quicker Clay is safely buried, the sooner we get moving!'

Although chastened, Vance still had the cojones to mention one other matter. 'What about his boots? Seems kind of a waste to put them under the ground as well.'

Taw clenched his ham like fists with unmistakable anger. 'I was with him when he paid cash money for them. They stay with him and that's an end to it. Don't press me further.'

Vance regarded him in guarded silence for a moment, before he and the six other remaining scavengers dismounted. Drawing their knives, they began to cut through the sod to excavate a rough and ready grave.

'Oh and in case any of you witless varmints didn't realize it, a decade is ten years,' Taw added sharply. 'That's a long time to ride with a man.'

★　★　★

John Clemens regarded the diminished group of fugitives with a snort of satisfaction. Then his spyglass settled on Cathy and his powder-stained forehead creased into a deep frown. Superficially, she appeared to be unhurt. Her hands definitely weren't tied and unlike her kidnappers she remained mounted. So why the hell didn't she just take off, back towards the Breaks?

Deciding that it was time to give the poor fools another demonstration of his prowess, he withdrew the Sharps from its scabbard and slung it over his shoulder. Taking hold of his horse's bridle, he firmly urged the animal backwards and down, so that in mere seconds it lay on the ground, effectively invisible to anyone more than a few yards away. Locating himself on the beast's neck, just above its withers, Clemens then had a perfect elevated firing position.

As he again raised the ladder sights, the concealed assassin pondered on whether to drop the gang's leader, but eventually decided against it. That was one man he needed to encounter close up, but only on his terms and with all the others dead. Even if the big oaf wouldn't beg for mercy, he would knowingly stare death in the face. Chuckling with anticipation, Clemens retracted the hammer and went through the so very familiar routine of taking another life.

★　★　★

Taw reflectively patted the fresh earth as he made his final farewells. Even though wood was available from the redundant travois, he had decided against any kind of marker. Other travellers seeing such a thing might decide to become 'resurrectionists', in the hope of finding a few coins or a saleable set of teeth.

'We need to go, boss,' Vance ventured insistently. Clambering to his feet, he abruptly staggered under the brutal assault of a heavy calibre rifle bullet, as it punched through his chest. 'Sweet Jesus, I'm kilt,' he proclaimed in absolute horror, before shock took over and robbed him of any further speech. Coughing blood, the fatally hit outlaw pirouetted slightly before collapsing on to the grass.

The only other person standing tall was Cathy and thus Taw yelled out, 'Get down while I try to locate him.'

So saying, he pointed his battered spyglass to the north and carefully scrutinized the landscape. Even with open grassland for thousands of yards, there was no indication of the whereabouts of the man hunter. It was both baffling and terrifying in equal measure.

Despite the chill, Taw's body was damp with sweat as he strained for a sign . . . any sign. Then he saw it. An unnatural mound in the grass. The haunches of an animal on its side.

'God damn, but he's good,' the outlaw muttered.

Lowering the glass, he peered round at his six remaining men. They gazed at him expectantly. When it came to the crunch, they had always expected him to come up with an answer and always in the past he had managed it. Yet his band's drastic depletion suggested that he might be losing his sure touch. A woman could do that to a man!

Struggling to shake off his uncharacteristically defeatist mood, Taw came to a decision. The time had come to make a stand and Vance's corpse gave him an idea.

'Right, listen up. Cut one of those travois loose.' Even as he spoke, Taw was crawling over to the still warm body. Steeling himself, he dipped his hand in the fresh blood and daubed it over his face and jacket. 'That bastard knows he's got a kill lying here. Only thing is, it's going to be me.'

Ignoring the shock on Cathy's face, he settled his gaze on her and continued, 'I need you to ride between him and us. Spoil his aim while everyone else mounts up and gets Vance on a horse. Poor bastard's going to have to come back to life for just a little while. You boys use the rawhide from the travois to tie his feet together and after that, place the frame over me, as though you couldn't risk the time for another burial. After my mistake with Clay, Clemens'll likely fall for it. Then you all ride like the devil is after you. Because if this doesn't work out, he definitely will be. Savvy?'

★　★　★

John Clemens slid another cartridge into the breech and prepared for a second shot. Unless the survivors intended remaining on their bellies until nightfall, he expected to drop at least one more as they mounted up. Then, much to his amazement, his wife urged her horse over, so that they were directly between him and the outlaws. After that he could only watch with increasing frustration as they clambered into their saddles. One man seemed to require a deal of assistance, but eventually they all rode off, with Cathy remaining at the rear.

'God damn it, what's got into that silly bitch?' he demanded loudly.

As though offering an opinion, his horse whinnied, thereby reminding him that there was really no longer any need for them to continue hugging the ground. Clambering to his feet, Clemens took a reflective chew on some beef jerky and waited patiently until the survivors had disappeared from view. Only then did he mount up and set off expectantly towards yet another patch of blood-soaked earth. As he got nearer, he noticed that a travois had been abandoned. It would have provided the makings for a nice fire, had he been prepared to allow himself one. Then he spotted the body beneath it and he smiled. That was another son of a bitch who wouldn't be robbing honest folk.

Taw Johnson sensed rather than heard the horseman approach. His left hand gripped the side of the travois, ready to hurl it aside, whilst his right clutched an Army Colt, cocked and ready. He knew full well the quality of the man that he was up against and so his flesh crawled with anticipation. The gunplay, when it happened, would likely be all over in a matter of seconds and if he failed, he didn't hold out much hope for the rest of his gang. Or, quite possibly, even Cathy. The approaching animal snickered slightly, as though pouring scorn on his efforts. Its hoofs were getting close now. It was time!

9

The surrounding landscape was apparently empty and only a solitary dead man awaited him, but nevertheless Clemens's Schofield was out of its holster. Having yet again restlessly scanned the horizon, he finally allowed his eyes to settle on the body underneath the travois. A man with his background was unlikely to take anything for granted and his heart suddenly lurched with shock. Something was very wrong and could be summed up in one word. Boots! Who would leave a pair of valuable boots on a cadaver?

Even as he levelled his revolver at the frame, a powerful arm hurled it to one side and the 'corpse' aimed a gun of its own. The order of fire was too close to call. Both weapons belched forth lead and each one drew blood. Taw roared with pain as a bullet ripped into his left shoulder, but he had been shot before and so somehow managed to keep hold of his Colt.

Clemens felt a burning pain lance into the side of his head and swayed backwards in the saddle. His horse, although well trained, reared up in alarm. The man hunter instinctively realized that if he remained mounted, he was finished and so kicked out of his stirrups and tumbled to the ground. Grunting at the jarring impact, he rolled once and then attempted to take a snap shot at his opponent. Except that with blurred vision and blood flowing over his face he couldn't see properly so he did the only thing left to him. Firing once for effect, he then kept on twisting and rolling in the long grass like an eel.

Feeling light-headed with pain, Taw managed to scramble around behind the discarded travois. Even as he did so, the Schofield crashed out again, sending a bullet into one of the side poles. Splinters narrowly missed him as he in turn fired at the maniac squirming in the grass.

'Do you hear that?' Cathy shouted at her six remaining companions. 'They're fighting each other. We have to go and help.'

Davis regarded her suspiciously. 'Yeah, but just who are you fixing to help, bitch? That's your husband out there, remember?'

She glowered at him in frustration. 'Let's just say that I've realized I married the wrong man, but if we don't hurry it might be too late to do anything about it.'

Still Davis and the others wavered.

'Sweet Jesus,' she cried out. 'If you sons of bitches won't go back, at least give me a gun.'

Finally, her entreaties took effect. The scavengers looked sheepishly at each other and Davis shrugged. 'Oh, what the hell,' he muttered. 'He'd do it for us, wouldn't he? And for Christ's sake, someone give her a gun. With luck, she'll shoot herself in the mouth.'

One of the others reluctantly handed Cathy a spare revolver, of which by then they sadly had many. His accompanying words were loaded with menace. 'Just make sure you point that in the right direction, lady. I've never actually kilt a female before, but I'll happily pop a cap on you if you play us false!'

Another gunshot ominously rang out and with that they turned in unison and urged their tired horses into motion. Despite their change of heart, the scavengers were noticeably reluctant and it wasn't long before Cathy had left them well behind.

John Clemens had managed to crawl back into undisturbed grass, which effectively made him invisible to the injured outlaw but, along with his own wound, unfortunately meant that he couldn't finish the job. Desperately, he used a kerchief to mop the blood from his eyes. Although he was bleeding profusely, the damage seemed to be superficial and in any case, he had another problem on his mind. His biggest vulnerability was that he should find himself on foot!

Taw Johnson's left shoulder was throbbing abominably and he was struggling to focus. Yet his next target didn't require a keen eye. A full-grown horse was only a little less difficult to hit than the side of a barn. Steeling himself against an unpleasant task, he fired off two shots into the belly of Clemens's animal. The poor beast emitted an almost human scream and promptly keeled over. Then, as though in answer to his prayers, he heard the sound of pounding hoofs.

Clemens swore viciously as he witnessed the bloody demise of his faithful animal. Its death meant that if he were to survive this encounter, he would have to start treading dangerously. His habit of always wearing full bandoliers meant that he still possessed plenty of ammunition, but he had to recover his rifle. Drawing in a deep breath, he suddenly launched himself to his feet and raced towards his belongings. As he dropped down next to the 'flesh and blood' barricade, one more shot crashed out from behind the travois. Untouched by the projectile, he seized the Sharps from its scabbard. Only then did he hear the sound that had brought joy to his opponent's heart.

Frantically peering through one unbloodied eye, Clemens twitched with surprise at the sight of his wife galloping towards the desperate conflict. Even more astonishing was the fact that she possessed a gun. As she careered up behind his wounded opponent, Clemens bellowed out, 'Shoot him!'

Cathy glanced sharply over at him, but instead of obeying his command she kept riding until her horse was directly between the two men. It didn't escape her husband's quick wits that such behaviour was becoming a nasty habit.

'What the hell are you about?' he barked out. 'He means to finish me!'

Rather than immediately answer, she merely gazed down on him, as though having just encountered him for the first time. Her features held a strangely unwelcoming expression, which did nothing to dispel his anxiety. He could only think that a fall or some such had scrambled her brains, because his head wound was not that disfiguring.

'God's blood, woman. It's me, John, your husband. Surely you must recognize me?'

Finally she displayed some recognition, but what came next gave him little comfort.

'Just go, John. Leave while you can, before the others catch up.'

'What the hell do you mean, go? I've come for you. I've *killed* for you.'

She favoured him with a sad smile. 'Oh, I've seen what you've done. I've discovered the kind of person you really are and I want nothing more to do with you. I'm staying with this man and I won't let you kill him.'

Stunned disbelief gradually changed to a sneering understanding. 'So that's it. You've turned whore and joined up with this border trash.' With the sound of more horses approaching, he momentarily fell silent and considered his options.

Time was short. There really was only one choice.

Rising up from behind his dead animal, he swiftly advanced on his wife, all the while taking care to keep her between him and her new *friend*.

'Get off the horse, now!' he barked.

With discomforting determination, she swung her revolver over to point it at his chest. He really didn't have time for all this.

'You won't shoot me,' he remarked with studied calm. 'We're still married, remember?' So saying, he reached out and firmly took the reins from her grasp. Then, before she could react, he slipped her foot out of the stirrup and heaved her bodily off the horse, ensuring that she fell in front of the outlaw leader.

'You pig,' she howled out in shock and anger.

With his Sharps securely over his shoulder, Clemens leapt up into the saddle and viciously dug his heels in. A band of riders was coming up fast, but as yet no one had opened fire and Taw Johnson couldn't draw a bead for fear of hitting Cathy. Even as Clemens raced away, half-blinded and desperately trying to control his unfamiliar mount, he still managed to have the last word.

'You'd better make the best of him, bitch, because this doesn't end here!'

Davis and the others had been in no 'all fired' hurry to overhaul Cathy, but now that they saw a flesh and blood enemy riding away, they got the bit between their teeth and eagerly chased after him. Only Jed, pale-faced and in great pain from his broken leg, rejoined his leader. As Taw staggered to his feet with Cathy's help, he yelled after them, 'Come back here, you fools!' But if any of them heard him, they affected not to.

'God damn it all to hell,' the outlaw raged. 'They haven't got the sense they were born with. They ought to join the cavalry!'

The three of them watched helplessly as the horsemen receded across the sea of grass. Taw knew exactly what was going to happen and sure enough it did. There was a distant crash and one of the men was flung backwards off his horse. The remaining *four* riders grabbed the reins of yet another spare animal and rapidly retraced their steps.

'If any of us are going to survive this, you need to start doing precisely what I say,' Taw hollered at them as they despondently reined up before him.

'Yeah, yeah,' agreed Davis grudgingly as he dismounted. It was plain for all to see that Taw was wounded and in pain and the scavenger sensed weakness. 'So what do we do now, boss? What fine orders have you got for us, that just might could parole that stinking gun hand to Jesus? That's if you should manage to plug the bleeding in your shoulder?' Even as he finished speaking, it occurred to him that he'd possibly pushed his luck too far.

Cathy was in the process of easing his jacket off, but Taw brushed her away and fiercely advanced on the other man. Davis was tall, but scrawny and singularly lacking in power. He belatedly recognized that even wounded, his leader would be too much to handle and so he backed off . . . but not fast enough.

Taw delivered a stinging open handed slap across Davis's face. He would happily have shot him as an example to the others, but he had lost far too many men as it was.

'The next time, I'll use my fist,' he growled. 'And then these boys'll need a shovel to scrape you up.'

As the smarting and embarrassed outlaw stared sullenly at him, Taw addressed the rest of the men. 'Let there be an end to this. If we get to fighting amongst ourselves, Clemens won't even need that god damned buffalo gun of his.' He paused to let his words sink in, before continuing. 'Now the way I see it, we need to get to a town.'

One of the others gazed at him warily. 'I don't like towns, boss . . . unless I'm looting them.'

Taw sighed. 'I know, I know. But I've

got lead in this shoulder that needs digging out and Jed's leg requires setting properly, or he'll be a cripple for the rest of his days. *And* we need to get out of sight of that maniac back there . . . at least until we're ready to have another crack at him.'

Curiosity got the better of Davis. 'So where are you thinking of taking us?'

Eager to heal any rifts, Taw patted him companionably on the shoulder. 'There's a small town to the south-east of here, called Roy. I don't know anything about it, other than it exists, but since there's nothing else for miles in any direction, it'll have to do.'

★   ★   ★

John Clemens ducked his head into the rock pool's icy water and immediately felt revived. He had temporarily retreated to the edge of the Breaks to regroup. His wound was clean and unlikely to infect and he had dispatched yet another of the shit-faced scavengers, but there was no room in his heart for any satisfaction. All he felt was burning rage.

After years of killing, both man and beast, he had finally settled down on his own spread with the woman of his dreams and then it had all been taken away from him. Well, he was going to ensure that the rest of those pestilential desperados were wiped off the face of the earth. With her new lover dead and gone, his whore of a wife could then plead to be taken back. What he hadn't yet decided was whether he would accept her. Maybe it would just be better to erase her from his memory and obtain another mail order bride from back East. Of course, to avoid being a bigamist, it would mean having to consign Cathy to hell along with the big outlaw!

* * *

Jared Tunstall regarded the set of newly fashioned horseshoes with satisfaction. He took pride in his job and as the town's only blacksmith, a great many people relied on his skill. Mopping his brow, the powerfully muscled tradesman stepped out of the smithy on to Roy's main and indeed only dirt street. He drew in the cold air with a pleasure that most people wouldn't comprehend, unless they happened to spend most of their working lives next to a furnace.

Gazing around, Jared took in the few clapboard buildings that lined either side of the thoroughfare. The small settlement was completely isolated in an undulating sea of grassland. Roy only survived because a few local ranchers and settlers needed somewhere to purchase supplies. It wasn't even important enough to merit the cost of a telegraph connection. As for the railroad, that might as well have existed in another century. Freight wagons were the only regular source of contact with the outside world.

And yet, the slow and predictable pace of life held great appeal for the blacksmith, because it hadn't always been so. Even twenty-three years after it finished, the blood-soaked War Between the States still came back to haunt his dreams and the intervening period had also often been far from peaceful. Stretching his massive frame, Jared turned back to the many tasks that awaited him by the forge. As he did so, he happened to glance to the north and what he saw brought a deep frown to his features.

A band of seven riders was slowly approaching the town and the blacksmith knew immediately that they weren't from any of the local ranches. Strangers, especially in such numbers, were extremely rare in Roy. With his work temporarily forgotten, Jared closely scrutinized the newcomers. Other than registering surprise at the presence of an obviously attractive woman, he didn't like what he saw. The men looked ragged and disreputable. They smelled of trouble with a capital T.

As the strangers drew nearer, he

observed that at least two of them appeared to be injured, which was another bad omen. Glancing around him, Jared noticed that a few other citizens had spotted the new arrivals, but that they were nervously keeping their distance.

'Some things never change,' he muttered to himself.

★　★　★

As the dog-tired group closed in on the small community, Taw addressed the others softly. 'We don't want any trouble here, so leave the talking to me.'

They were all aware of the immense figure in a blacksmith's apron apparently waiting for them on the main street.

'He must be hoping for some business,' Davis remarked dryly, but then caught Taw's sharp eye and nodded silently.

It was obvious that the big man wasn't intending to step aside and so before long, the scavengers reined up directly in front of him. Although the blacksmith wasn't wearing a gun, the meeting had all the hallmarks of a confrontation, which was the last thing that Taw wanted.

'You folks look a mite ill used,' remarked Jared mildly, as he struggled to keep his eyes off the female.

'Ain't that the truth, mister,' responded Taw, equally softly. Being merely wounded and dog-tired rather than stupid, he had not missed the other man's preoccupation.

For an achingly long moment nobody else spoke, until Jared suddenly favoured Cathy with a broad smile and knuckled his forehead.

'My name's Jared Tunstall, miss. I'm the town blacksmith, by trade. What brings you all to Roy?'

Cathy returned his smile, but mindful of Taw's instructions, remained silent. The outlaw leader was quick to respond.

'We had a run in with some real mean hombres, who kind of took against us up in the Breaks,' that man replied. 'I caught a bullet in the shoulder and Jed here has got a broke leg. We could use some doctoring and a place to hole up for a spell.'

Jared nodded coolly, the woman temporarily forgotten. What he said next was deliberately calculated to provoke a reaction. 'I've heard that the Breaks is a refuge for all sorts of people on the dodge. You were lucky that nobody was killed. We don't see many bullet wounds around here. It'll likely put a strain on our horse doctor.' He paused, before adding sharply, 'I didn't get your name, mister.'

'Probably because he didn't give it,' snarled Davis with unconcealed venom. 'What's it to you who and what we are, anyway?'

Jared's eyes narrowed slightly as he took in the unrestrained hostility. He knew full well what these men were: scoundrels on the run, who very likely deserved everything that happened to them. The only thing that puzzled him was the girl's involvement. She looked far too clean and respectable to be a 'Dutch Gal'. What he said next came as something of a surprise, as had been intended.

'Because I'm also the town marshal . . . when there's a call for such a thing, which ain't often around these parts.'

'Huh, I might have known,' grunted Davis. 'A law dog!'

'Shut your mouth!' Taw growled menacingly at him, before allowing his hard eyes to lock on those of the marshal. His shoulder throbbed abominably and he knew that if he didn't dismount soon, he would quite likely just topple into the dirt. Nevertheless, a faint smile played on his lips as he responded wearily, 'Believe me, Marshal, we *really* ain't looking for any trouble. We've had more than our fair share lately. And we ain't looking for handouts, either. We've got money for the sawbones and room and board.'

Jared nodded slowly. 'Fair enough, but you'll find accommodation pretty sparse around here. No hotel and only a very few spare rooms to speak of. I can maybe organize a place for the lady to stay, but you fellas'll have to bed down in the livery. It's the largest building we've got.' Gesturing down the street, he added, 'You head on over there and get situated, while I locate the doc.' So saying, he finally backed off towards the smithy. All the while, his eyes stayed on the newcomers as they urged their weary mounts towards the livery stables. It occurred to him that it was very probably time to locate his badge and gun.

'I don't like that big son of a bitch,' Davis muttered quietly out of the corner of his mouth.

'Thank God you didn't let him see it,' Taw replied drily.

10

Marshal Jared Tunstall took a number of Roy's citizens by surprise the following morning, as he strode out of the smithy. Many of them couldn't actually remember when they had last seen him wearing both a badge *and* gun. His Remington revolver, many a lawman's weapon of choice, nestled snugly in a polished black holster. Hanging from a well maintained gun belt, it seemed a little at odds with his rough working clothes.

Not possessing a jailhouse or office of any kind, he lived in a single room built on to the rear of his smithy. All his meals were taken out, at an eating house further down the street. He led a solitary life and there could be no denying that Jared was, on occasion, a very lonely man. It was this, as much as any official business, which prompted him to pay a visit on the very attractive young lady now rooming above McLean's General Store. She had been on his mind throughout a long and restless night, because it was a sad fact that in Roy's small population, there wasn't another unattached female to match her in looks. Whether she was available or not was entirely another matter.

As he tentatively knocked on her door, he felt an unaccustomed flutter of unease in his belly. What if she wasn't alone? What if one of those saddle tramps had sneaked up the back stairs without being spotted by Missus McLean's eagle eye? He had seen the way the big man with the shoulder wound had looked at her and how his eyes rarely left her. And then she opened the door, favoured him with a genuine smile of welcome and all his nerves disappeared . . . for a brief moment.

'I'm real sorry to trouble you, miss. Only I feel it's my certain duty to ask you a few questions.'

Cathy peered up at his open, honest features and formed an immediate liking for him. Strangely enough, he reminded her of her late pa. He too had been a man that worked with his hands. Had he not died before his time of smallpox, she might not have ended up in a doubtful relationship with an outlaw, whilst fleeing from her rightful husband.

'I can see how you might have some concerns,' she lightly replied, opening the door wider to allow him entry. Although not having visited the bath-house yet, she had washed her face and vigorously brushed the trail dust out of her clothes. The attention and exercise was enough to provide her with a radiance that brought an ache to the marshal's heart.

After crowding his massive frame into the small room, he stood there uncomfortably or a moment, very conscious of her lovely eyes resting on his. Not wanting to stare too obviously at her, he briefly took in his surroundings. The clapboard walls were unplastered and unadorned and the only light came from a minute window that sorely needed washing. He couldn't help but think that she suited altogether better surroundings.

Finally, after swallowing heavily, he got some words together. 'If you don't mind me saying, miss, you appear a mite out of place with those . . . the men that you arrived with. Could it be that your movements are not entirely free?'

She favoured him with a sad smile that made him want to wrap his bear-like arms around her, which of course wouldn't do at all. Desperately ploughing on, he added, 'What I'm trying to say is, if they're holding you against your will, then now is the time to tell me. Even if they don't break the law in Roy, I can at least send them on their way without you.'

Cathy's eyes widened expressively. 'You'd do that for me? They're dangerous men, you know.'

Back on safer ground, he nodded grimly. 'Oh, I don't doubt that, but I've had *my* moments as well!'

Her mouth opened and then closed again in silence, as she pondered his offer. She barely knew this part-time lawman and yet there seemed to be something basically decent about him. Yes, he apparently found her attractive, but she perceived that that wasn't the only motive behind his presence in her room. It appeared that he possessed a sense of duty as well. Finally, some sixth sense prompted her to tell him everything and it took quite some time.

Jared's features registered incredulity as he absorbed her remarkable story. 'So this husband of yours is very likely to be still out there,' he remarked after Cathy had eventually finished.

She nodded. 'He never gives up. And I can't help thinking that I'm partly to blame.'

Feeling suddenly very protective of the young woman, Jared was quick to scoff at that. 'Oh, so it's your fault you got kidnapped by a gang of desperados, after Clemens left you all alone in a frontier cabin? I don't think so.' He paused for a moment, while he pondered his next move. Given the danger that the men represented, there really wasn't any choice in the matter, but it gave him chance to remain close to her for a little longer.

At last he sighed and announced his intentions. 'It's my duty to the citizens of this town to get Taw Johnson and his riff raff out of here as soon as possible. I'm going over to the livery to see when they'll be fit to ride. When they leave, it'll be up to you whether you go with them. But think on this. Johnson is known throughout the territory as a bad hombre and winter's upon us. That's a bad combination for a young lady such as you. Whatever affection that you think you feel for him may not survive his lifestyle and if you're off in the wilderness when you discover it, things may go badly for you.'

With that, he turned away and reached for the door latch.

'Thank you, Marshal,' Cathy murmured softly and then he was gone.

Whatever else his visit had achieved, it had given her a great deal to think on.

As Jared stepped from the shelter of the building on to the street, two things occurred. A flurry of snowflakes came out of the leaden sky and then just as quickly died away, but there could be no doubt that there would be a substantial covering before nightfall.

'Marvellous,' he decided sourly to himself. 'That's all we need right now.'

Then, as he glanced over at the livery, one of the big doors eased open and one of Johnson's 'scum' wandered around to the north-facing side of the building. Unbuttoning his trousers, the scruffy individual began to urinate with great satisfaction on to the timber wall.

'God damn it all to hell,' snarled Jared. 'You there!' he bellowed out. 'We have ladies in this town.'

The other man merely smirked and retorted, 'Well then, send them over here. I've got something for them to feast on!'

Jared felt a tightness in his chest as

real anger began to build within him. He had never tolerated that kind of behaviour in his town and he wasn't about to start. Clenching his huge fists, he strode purposefully across the thoroughfare. As he closed in on the uncouth lout, that man's brutalized features twisted into a mixture of belligerence and fear. The blacksmith/lawman had to be the biggest creature he'd seen that wasn't covered in body fur. Bigger than his boss by far.

'My town doesn't possess a jailhouse, so you're just gonna have to take a beating,' the marshal stated with the unnerving assurance of someone very capable of doing just that. Yet before he could even make a move, an unseen force swept in from the north.

The scavenger slammed forward into the wall, all traces of hostility abruptly gone. They were replaced by a graphic display of agony and shock that caused the startled lawman to momentarily freeze. He didn't need to hear the distant report that followed on, to know that the miscreant had been shot, but it had been a considerable time since he had actually witnessed such thing. Then, as hard learned professionalism kicked in, Jared came to his senses. Realizing that it was pointless to reach for his own weapon, he instead grabbed his erstwhile prey and heaved him over his right shoulder. Even as he did so, the wounded man coughed blood on to the street and groaned weakly. Moving fast, Jared got around the corner to relative safety and made for the livery's entrance. His peripheral vision informed that a number of townspeople were staring at him in stunned surprise.

Taw Johnson twitched nervously as something heavy thumped against the stable wall. He was in a strange limbo land between sleep and consciousness, but the sound of a far-off gunshot abruptly banished that. Attempting to get to his feet, he grunted with pain and merely had to settle for lifting his head off the hay. Having had a large piece of lead removed from his shoulder the previous evening, any other movement was just too excruciating. Then the stable door was unceremoniously booted open and he instinctively knew that the spell of peace that he had hoped for in Roy was irrevocably shattered.

Marshal Tunstall gently laid his trembling burden on a bed of hay and looked around. Thankfully, the horse doctor had conveniently stopped by to inspect his human patients, although Jared doubted very much if anything could be done for the latest one.

'Another bullet wound, doc. For what it's worth, I reckon this one looks fatal.'

A hunched, bespectacled figure in a badly worn black frock coat stepped out of the shadows and knelt down next to the trembling scavenger. The doctor, a man by the name of Curren, was possibly in his mid-forties, but appeared far older. He seemed to be permanently cloaked with an air of anguish, which wasn't really warranted from only dealing with the needs of animals. As the dying man shuddered and clutched at his arm, the sawbones glanced up at the town marshal.

'As usual, you're not wrong, Jared. But what's occurring here? What has brought all this violence amongst us?'

Rather than answer directly, Jared switched his attention to Taw's supine figure.

'It's him, isn't it? John Clemens has trailed you here and now it's all starting again. How many were you originally, fifteen?'

Taw momentarily closed his eyes, as though absorbing the horror that just wouldn't go away. Then he peered over at the bulky figure, taking in both his badge and gun belt. Despite the parlous situation, he wasn't prepared to 'eat dirt' from some two-bit law dog.

'I see the blacksmith's taken the day off and the marshal's been busy,' he remarked with heavy sarcasm. 'You've obviously had a long talk with Cathy. Pretty, isn't she?'

Jared stared down at him grim faced.

'By Cathy, you mean *Missus Clemens*. The kidnapped wife of the man that's hunting you down like dogs. Seems like poetic justice to me. Except that now, it's happening in *my* town.'

Aware that his *four* remaining men were watching him closely, Taw made a supreme effort and using the wall of one of the stalls, managed to drag himself upright. With sweat streaming from his face, he snarled. 'Well, I'm all broken up about that, Mister Lawman. Question is, what do you propose to do about it?'

Jared glanced around at the five unwanted newcomers and came to a decision. To be honest, he'd actually made it just after he'd stepped out of Cathy's room, but he wouldn't have cared to admit that in front of any of his fellow townspeople *or* the watching outlaws. And besides, the shooting had changed everything.

'If I really tried, I could probably find some wanted papers on you. Trouble is, we don't have a jail and the circuit judge hardly ever comes here. So I want you all on your horses and out of here, now!'

Taw recoiled slightly, but recovered fast. 'What, even him?' he sneered, gesturing towards his fading companion.

Jared glanced dismissively at the blood-soaked man struggling through death's door. 'All he's destined for is a cold hole in the ground . . . if he's got the spondulix to pay for it. My only concern is for the good people of this town. That sharpshooter out there has got this place squarely in his sights.'

Despite his weakened condition, Taw's wits were far from addled. Wiping the sweat from his eyes, he shot a meaningful glance at his men and retorted, 'Just to get things right in my mind, are you ordering Cathy out of town as well, or does she get special treatment?'

A vein bulged in Jared's forehead. He didn't take such backtalk from anybody, especially as he didn't really have an impartial answer. And yet he wasn't so angry as to not recognize that he was being baited . . . for a purpose. There were now only three able-bodied men remaining out of the gang that had originally dropped down over the Canadian border, but their opinion of the law hadn't improved any. They were bunched together off to his right and the lean, mean-looking individual who had previously called him a law dog, appeared to be the most trigger happy.

Apparently on the point of tackling Johnson, the massive lawman abruptly turned and launched himself at Davis. Reacting fast, that man went for his six-gun, but had barely cleared leather before his assailant reached him. Using his left hand, Jared seized his victim by the throat and then swung around behind him. Next, with his right hand, he grabbed Davis's gun hand in a vicelike grip and dragged him bodily backwards.

The helpless man's two cronies drew their weapons, but with the lawman using him as a human shield they had no safe shot. And then Jared began to contract his left hand. With his face turning crimson, Davis frantically kicked and struggled, but he had no chance against the marshal's bear-like strength. It was then pathetically easy for the lawman to relieve him of his weapon, which he conveniently used to cover the others.

'Drop those guns or I snap his windpipe like a twig,' came the graphic ultimatum.

The two men glanced at their boss for assistance, but that individual was barely able to remain upright. His shoulder was throbbing something terrible. During the extraction, he had lost a lot of blood and all he really wanted to do was lie down in the hay. Jed would be no help, either. His leg had been painfully set using wooden splints and he was still drugged up on laudanum. Very reluctantly, they eased the hammers down and placed their revolvers on the ground. Jared nodded with grim satisfaction and relaxed his left hand slightly.

'I'll say it again,' he rasped harshly. 'I want all of you on horseback and out of my town, now!'

Nobody moved, probably because only two of the five were able and they were waiting on instructions from their boss. Taw Johnson shook his head with resigned frustration.

'You wouldn't have the upper hand if I wasn't wounded,' he commented bitterly.

That cut no ice with the lawman. 'Maybe so, but I have and you are!'

A strained silence fell on the livery stables, broken only by the sounds of animals chomping on their feed in the various stalls. Suddenly, one of the heavy main doors began to open, which only served to heighten the tension. Cathy, her lovely features contorted by anxiety, peered into the vast interior. Fresh snowflakes lay on her shoulders.

'I thought I heard a shot. It sounded far away, which made me think of . . . ' She fell silent, as her eyes settled on the bloodied outlaw.

'He's just passed,' announced the doctor sadly, quite possibly because there would be no fee. He paused as though coming to a decision. Then to everybody's surprise, and with his eyes blazing, Roy's only medical man suddenly drew himself erect and advanced on Jared. 'I know that this mess is none of your doing, Marshal, but I can't allow you to go making it into something worse than it already is. There'll be snow coating the land by nightfall. If you force these wounded men out there now, they'll surely die. You're a tough man by any reckoning, but I never took you for a cold-blooded murderer.'

With his hand still around someone's throat, such an accusation was not that fanciful, but Jared was surprised nonetheless. He stared wide-eyed at the doctor whilst carefully re-assessing the situation.

'Oh, I'm no murderer,' he finally replied. 'But maybe I see things from a darker standpoint than you. If I sit back and do nothing, you could end up with more patients than you can handle and some of them might well be your fellow citizens. So this is my last word. The two wounded can stick around under your tender care until they're as fit as rutting bucks, but these other three leave now.'

It was Davis who first realized the lethal implications of such an arrangement. Although immobile in Jared's grip, he was still able to find his tongue. 'Sweet Jesus, if you send us out there now, that kill crazy maniac'll have us for sure. At least wait until dark, so he won't see us.'

Jared spun the man around and pushed him back to rejoin his cronies. His deadpan response contained chilling logic. 'No can do. I need him to see you pull out. That way it may draw him after you and buy us some time. That's a single shot Sharps he's using, so if you ride full chisel, he'll only likely nail one of you. Three to one odds is the best deal you're going to get from me, *whatever* the doc says.'

Even though massaging his throat, Davis still had the *cojones* to resist. 'And what if we just flat out won't go? Then what?'

The part-time marshal displayed growing impatience. 'I'll have you tied on your horses. You're keeping me from my proper job and I'm getting bored with all this.'

'*He's getting bored*,' the outlaw announced incredulously as he turned to his leader. 'Are you going to let him do this, boss?'

Taw grimaced weakly. 'It doesn't look like I've got a lot of choice. We seem to have stirred up a real shit storm, don't we, boys?'

That was just too much for Davis. 'You mean *you did* when you kidnapped this piece of ass. She's cost us more dead than those poxy Mounties ever did. We should have just all taken turns and then sent her back to that crazy son of a bitch.'

'Oh, and what would have stopped

him,' retorted Taw scornfully. 'Don't you understand? He's not interested in her anymore. He's just doing what he knows best . . . killing!'

The gunshot crashed out in the confined space, shocking all but one of those present. Even as the bullet tore up compacted dirt at Davis's feet, Jared surged forward and tapped Davis sharply on the side of his head with the smoking gun barrel.

'I don't care to hear that kind of talk about Cathy,' he growled menacingly.

'Oh, it's Cathy now, is it?' the outlaw foolishly responded. Everyone completely missed the look of surprise that passed across Taw's features.

'You just don't know when to hush up, boy,' Jared hissed through clenched teeth. Davis's features turned ashen, as the warm muzzle was rammed under his chin and the hammer retracted. Genuinely believing that his time was up, the luckless scavenger abruptly lost all control of his bladder. As the ground at their feet turned to mush, the marshal glanced disdainfully at him. 'Enough of all this piss and vinegar,' he decreed. 'The three of you mount up, now!'

11

John Clemens carefully scrutinized the large building through his spyglass. He lay flat out in the grass at the top of a small rise, some 600 yards north of the 'one horse' town. His mount was ground tethered behind and below him, out of sight of any prying eyes. After spending a cold night on the open plains, bleakly hunkered around a necessarily small fire, he had tracked the dwindling band of fugitives to Roy. Speculating that with two wounded men, they had most certainly travelled there intentionally and so were still around, the man hunter decided to watch and wait. It was then that he had got lucky. One of them had sauntered out of the stables and the sudden prospect of slaying an unsuspecting outlaw whilst he was taking a piss had greatly appealed to the assassin.

Strangely enough, Clemens had then looked on with an almost detached interest, as the dying outlaw had been carried back into the livery. Killing from a distance could have that effect on a man. But there was also an undeniable sense of satisfaction. It now seemed that he had called it correctly. The rest of his victim's cronies had to be holed up in there as well. The sight of his own worthless wife, hurrying over to the building to join her lover, only confirmed that fact. And so, when both big doors were heaved open simultaneously, he knew exactly what was happening. Some or all of them were making a break for it.

Dropping the spyglass like a hot coal, he grabbed the Sharps, which of course was already sighted for the correct distance and cocked. There were three riders; line abreast and all were frenetically urging their animals to speed. Clemens knew that he would get no more than one chance and then only because he was more or less behind them in line of sight, thereby helping to cancel out their rapid motion. Even so, there would be no time for a considered shot.

Tugging the butt into his shoulder, he took rapid aim at the rear of the middle horse. That way he also had an outside chance of tripping one of the flanking animals. The sharpshooter breathed in, held it and squeezed the trigger. With the powerful detonation still ringing in his ears, he then smoothly worked the well oiled under lever. As the smoke drifted clear, Clemens rapidly reloaded from the row of cartridges on the grass in front of him and then sighted down the thirty-inch barrel for his next shot.

The centre horse had lurched forward on to its knees, sending its rider crashing to the hard ground. One of the accompanying horsemen had only just kept control of his mount, as he desperately swung around the dying beast. As the two survivors raced off, heading south, Clemens had to choose between chancing a marginal shot at one of them or nailing the downed outlaw before he had the chance to reach cover. He chose the safe option.

Sheer terror brought Davis to his senses. With appalling pain lancing through his right leg and seemingly unable to get to his feet, he crawled clear of his thrashing horse. The livery doors were still open and so he struck out for them on all fours. With terrifying insight, he recognized the sheer futility of it, but a desperate urge to live kept him moving anyway. Glancing up, he caught sight of the 'law dog' impassively watching him from the threshold.

'God damn y — ' he began and then the .50 calibre bullet ripped into his upper body and suddenly he couldn't see or say anything at all.

Jared stared at Davis's broken body for a moment longer, before turning back to face the others. 'The gobshite didn't make it,' he reported dispassionately.

Doc Curren was very unimpressed with such an offhand report. 'You sent that man to his death, Jared Tunstall!'

The marshal favoured Cathy with a warm smile, as though exempting her from what he was about to say, before responding sharply, 'Never mind these no good yahoos. What about those folks out there? Your friends and neighbours. They've just watched two men get gunned down on their street by an unknown killer. A killer who's still got unfinished business. Don't you think they might be wondering when it's their turn?'

The other man recoiled slightly, as though not having even considered such a thing and Jared switched his attention to Taw Johnson. The outlaw had collapsed back on to the hay, but was viewing the lawman speculatively.

'The two men that just left. Are they gone for good or are they likely to hang around to see how things pan out?'

Taw snorted contemptuously. 'Those two? They'll be halfway to Mexico by now. Like we should have been, if we hadn't tangled with the wrong man.'

'That's what I figured,' Jared replied. 'Looks like I'd better tell the good citizens to stay off the street, because the way I see it, if Clemens decides not to follow them he'll be moving into town next.' With that, he turned away and strode towards the door.

Cathy was aghast. 'Surely you're not going out there, after what's just happened?'

'Way I figure it, your husband knows exactly what he's about. He'll know how many he's killed and run off and that there's just two wounded outlaws in this building. So when I walk out of here, standing tall, I'll be perfectly safe.' The town marshal sounded so confident that Cathy just shook her head in amazement. And yet, as he left the stables, she noticed that there was a tightness to his features that suggested he was in reality far from confident of the outcome.

'That's one very brave man,' she

commented, with a touch of awe in her voice that Taw Johnson couldn't fail to notice.

'Huh, he ain't so special,' he retorted. 'Back in the Breaks, I faced up to that Clemens bastard real good!'

Cathy regarded the wounded outlaw boss with mixed emotions. Although still feeling some regard for him, she heard the obvious jealousy and didn't care for it. Why did all the men in her life have to possess major character flaws?

★ ★ ★

At that very moment 'that Clemens bastard' was pondering his options. He had watched the massive individual stride, apparently fearlessly, across Roy's main thoroughfare and of course had held his fire. The random killing of a non-entity held no interest for him. There always had to be a reason.

He did his thinking on the move, having shifted position after the latest shootings. There was always a slim chance that some overeager citizens might decide to form a posse and try to rush his last location. With his remaining two victims wounded and apparently laid up in the stables, he had swung round to the southeast and increased the distance between him and the town so that he was out of sight of the rooftops. After riding for some time, he changed direction again and kept going until he was directly south of Roy.

He knew that sitting out on the plains no longer served any purpose. It was time to close in and finish the job. And besides, there was snow in the air. A blind man could smell it and Clemens had no desire to freeze his butt off out in the open, with no possibility of a warming fire. The question was how to enter the small town without drawing unwelcome attention. As far as he knew, neither of the outlaws had seen him close up, but after the recent murders the townsfolk would be suspicious of any more newcomers.

It was then that, with almost divine good timing, he suddenly became aware of a faint rumbling noise emanating from the south. The ever-suspicious assassin cocked his head and tried hard to place the sound. Then, as the distinctive noise grew nearer, a smile gradually formed on his hard features. He knew that the perfect solution to his problem was conveniently crawling straight towards him.

Swiftly making up his mind, Clemens unfastened the girth strap and heaved the saddle off his stolen horse. Next, he removed the cartridge bandoliers from around his torso. He had been wearing them for so long that he almost felt naked without them. Coiling them around the Sharps, he wrapped the whole lot up in his blanket. Anybody seeing the bundle would probably know that it contained a rifle, but not what type. Then, without any hesitation, he tightly seized hold of the reins, drew his knife and plunged the razor sharp blade deep into the unfortunate animal's neck. As blood sprayed everywhere, the poor creature screamed with shock and tried to bolt. Ignoring the gore, Clemens held on tight and sawed the vicious cutting edge back and forth, until his latest and most undeserving prey weakened and toppled to the ground.

It would have been far easier and certainly more humane to have just shot the beast, but that could have drawn unwelcome attention from the already nervous residents of the nearby town. Withdrawing the blade, he meticulously wiped it clean on the horse's trembling flanks, before tucking it back in its sheath. The bloodstains on his own clothes didn't concern him. He could easily explain those away by simply telling the truth!

The two freighters knew that they had almost reached the end of their journey. At last they could allow themselves to ponder the wondrous delights of a bathhouse, sleeping indoors and eating food cooked by someone else. It really didn't matter what it was, just so long as they didn't have to prepare it themselves. For many long, cold days they had been heading roughly due north from the Northern Pacific Railroad hub of Billings. They had a team of six mules hauling the two massive linked wooden freight wagons. Both were piled high with provisions secured under waterproof tarpaulins, all destined for the folks living in and around the town of Roy. The whole conveyance, which also served as a shelter for its operators, was like some monstrous land train creaking across the plains. Each night they slept under the cover of its solid wagon beds, relentlessly taking turns to stand guard duty.

Henry and Kyle Timmons were twin brothers who had been in the freight business for their whole adult lives. Although basically decent, no one could ever have accused them of being intelligent, and that fact was about to work against them. Now pushing fifty, grizzled and weather-beaten, they had so far survived the arrival of railroads in the remote territory and with the passing of any Indian threat, they were able to enjoy a relatively trouble free life in the open air. However, there was always the possibility of road agents and so when they saw a man alone in the distance, they instinctively reached for their sawn-off shotguns. Whilst there was only one stranger visible, there could easily be others, laying in wait in the long grass. As they gradually drew closer, Kyle noticed that a dead horse lay close by, which offered a reason for the man being on foot, but didn't do anything to allay their fears.

'Just you keep your hands clear of any weapons, mister,' he commanded loudly. 'Me and my brother both know how to use these scatterguns. Anybody tries to jump us and you get it first!'

Barely had the words left his lips, when the two freighters noticed the blood spattered over the stranger's well worn duds and they tightened their grip on the deadly weapons.

Their jumpiness had not gone unnoticed by John Clemens and he allowed his features to form a relaxed smile.

'Easy with those crowd-pleasers, boys. You don't have anything at all to fear from me. If the truth be told, I'm real glad to see you. This faithful old horse of mine stepped in a gopher hole a ways back and snapped a leg. It fair broke my heart to have to put him out of his misery. Looking at the state of me, I guess I should have used a cartridge, but I'm running a mite short on shells.'

Although their mule team was reacting nervously to the smell of fresh blood, the brothers glanced at each other and relaxed slightly.

'Reckon you could have saved yourself some trouble, mister,' Henry observed loudly over the constant creaking of the wagons timbers. 'With the wind behind me, I could almost spit to the nearest town from here.'

Clemens affected a convincing display of stunned astonishment as he called back, 'Sweet Jesus. You fellas are lifesavers. I thought I was miles from anywhere.'

206

Kyle offered an easy smile, his fears beginning to dissipate. 'There's a place called Roy, just over yonder a piece.' As the wagons finally came to a halt next to the stranded traveller he continued in a quieter tone, 'What brings you out here anyhow? You don't look like a rancher to me and I can't think of much else that'd bring a man out here in winter.'

The man hunter knew that this was his make or break moment. The shotguns were no longer pointed directly at him, but they were still cocked and ready. Consciously affecting an injured air, he smiled sadly and moved over to pat the nearest mule, but it shied away from the blood on his clothes.

'Well, you seem like decent folks to me,' he softly remarked. 'So I'll tell you the god's honest truth. I've got a small spread up north, beyond the Breaks. My wife's run off with a trader and I've come looking for them. I don't want no trouble. Just to have her back would be enough. We are lawful wedded and I've missed her something terrible. I was away buying supplies and I guess his soft talk and lies must have turned her senses.' With that, he shrugged and shook his head mournfully, yet all the time his sharp eyes never left the freighters.

The brothers stared at each other for a moment as though in silent communication and then nodded almost simultaneously. They carefully lowered the twin hammers on their weapons and placed them below the bench seat. It was Henry who had the words. 'Sounds like your life has been all shit an' no sugar lately. I guess the least we can do is give you a ride into Roy. There's snow coming and a man could freeze to death alone on these plains. Heave your saddle and possibles on to the wagon, if you can find a space and then join us on the bench.'

As he did as he was bidden, Clemens's smile was genuine and unforced. He made sure that the innocuous looking blanket roll was tucked under the saddle. Finally settling on the hard seat, he accepted a handshake from each man as they introduced themselves, before he responded.

'I'm right glad to make your acquaintance. My name is John and I'm beholden to you.'

Before they could enquire after his last name, he quickly moved on. 'If anybody should ask, I'd be much obliged if you'd tell them that I work for you. Just until I see whether my wife is in town. That way no one will ask why I am there, while I look for her. Would you do that for me?' Then, before they could answer, he added, 'Don't worry, you don't have to put me on wages. Ha ha.'

Henry and Kyle glanced searchingly at each other. They hadn't been raised to lie and were not always that adept at spotting such things from others. Finally they shrugged in unison, because most of the time they seemed to function like two halves of the same whole. It was the latter that responded.

'I guess it can't hurt any. Just don't put any drinks on our tab, huh?'

* * *

Taw Johnson glanced over at his sole remaining scavenger and favoured him with a weary smile. 'That bull-necked marshal might think this is his town, but I reckon that sharpshooter's going to be down our throats once it gets dark.' He had deliberately waited until Cathy had taken her leave, before saying such. Since arriving in Roy, he had noticed a change in her that he didn't like. Perhaps returning to civilization had altered her opinion of him or perhaps he'd just hoped for too much in the first place.

Jeb's mean looking features twisted with a mixture of pain and anger.

'After what he's done to me, I'd just like to get that bastard close up. Busted leg or not, I'll cut his liver out.' Then he looked questioningly at his leader.

210

'What are you thinking, boss?'

'That we need some height,' came the reply. For the first time since arriving there, Taw took a long, hard look at his surroundings. For such a small town, it was a very large building. Rectangular in shape, the rear two thirds of it had a long central isle with individual stalls on either side, many of which were occupied. Stretching above those was a hayloft, which was accessed by a wooden ladder in the big, open area at the front of the structure. Next to that was a rope and pulley system, used for heaving up bails of hay. Gesturing to the loft, he queried, 'You reckon you can get up there if I help?'

'Damn right I can,' Jeb snarled. 'It's time we were on the high ground!'

Taw peered over at the simple looking stable hand, who had somehow managed to keep clear of them ever since their arrival and was now lethargically raking some hay at the far end of the livery.

'We're going up into the loft for some

shuteye. You got a problem with that?'

The pimply young man quickly shook his head. He had no desire to tangle with those two ornery-looking fellas, wounded or not.

Jared Tunstall had returned to his primary occupation of blacksmith, albeit with his gun belt still buckled on. The bitter cold front was keeping Roy's citizens off the street and the sneaking assassin could literally be anywhere, so there was little point in patrolling some invisible perimeter. He would dearly have enjoyed visiting Missus Clemens again, in an unofficial capacity of course, but unaccustomed nerves had so far prevented that.

His hand had just grasped the bellows to pump up the furnace, when two things happened almost simultaneously. He heard the rumble of massive wagon wheels approaching and it began to snow, this time with serious intent. Propelled by a freezing north wind, big flakes whipped through the town. The blizzard effectively reduced visibility to a few feet. As the vague outline of a mule team came into view, Jared commented to himself, 'I'll bet those freighters are damn glad they've made town!'

He watched as the huge ethereal shape of the land train pulled up in front of McLean's General Store. Three ghostly shapes clambered down and moved under the awning of the building. It occurred to him that the Timmons brothers must have taken on some help, but saw nothing odd in that. As with everyone, they weren't getting any younger. With work still to finish, he vigorously pumped on the bellows and felt the heat increase in the furnace. No matter how much snow came down, he knew there was at least one man in town who would be keeping warm that night. Or so he thought!

A good few minutes would pass before he was assailed by a nagging doubt that was sufficiently strong to persuade him to follow in the tracks of the new arrivals.

12

The three men clustered under the awning, glad of the temporary reprieve from the weather.

'No point in trying to unload in this,' Henry commented ... or was it Kyle? Poor visibility or not, it was hard to tell between them. 'I don't know about anyone else, but I need a drink to cut through the phlegm.'

John Clemens had deliberately left his possessions on the wagon. He wanted to keep the Sharps out of sight and in any case, it was in his interests to stick with the freighters for a while longer.

'And I'm buying,' he proclaimed. 'It's the least I can do for you fellas. But for you two, I'd be stranded out on the plains in this, freezing my nuts off.'

There could be no argument with that and so the brothers led him along the street to Roy's only saloon. The cheery, comforting glow of lamplight seemed to draw them towards it like a magnet. As the three snow-covered men erupted into the smoke-fogged warmth, all heads turned to view the new arrivals.

'Well, hell, if it ain't the Timmons brothers,' proclaimed a pockmarked, beefy individual behind the bar. The grin that crossed his features was genuine and unforced. 'You sons of bitches certainly brought the weather with you and that's no error.'

There followed the usual exchange of friendly ribald banter, common amongst long-term acquaintances on the frontier. The saloon, with its two big iron stoves and tobacco-laden atmosphere, was quite obviously the focal point of the town. Only when the bonhomie had subsided slightly, did the tall and rangy, blood-spattered newcomer step from behind his *employers* to claim the room's full attention. Before anyone could comment, he sharply tapped the bar.

'Three whiskeys, bartender. And not the shit you serve tame Indians. The good stuff, down back of you.'

The Timmons brothers blinked with surprise, whilst the proprietor coloured angrily. Such confrontational talk was uncommon in a sleepy little town like Roy.

'For a stranger around here, you run your mouth kind of reckless, mister!'

Clemens leaned forward and for an apparently endless moment, fixed his hard eyes on the man. There could be no mistaking their latent menace, so much so that the recipient began to feel his palms growing clammy. The saloon-keeper had been around long enough to recognize the mark of a very dangerous man. He tried in vain to meet the stare.

Then, unexpectedly, the intimidating newcomer abruptly displayed a broad grin. 'Aw heck, mister. I'm just funning with you, is all. Me and my employers here have struggled across all of God's creation bringing supplies to this town. We must deserve some quality bug juice, don't your reckon?'

The other man had been desperately reaching for the shotgun under his counter and he heaved a sigh of relief at the sudden change of mood. Glancing around him at his regulars, he wondered how to hide the fact that he'd been serving them cheap 'rot gut' for so long. Grabbing another bottle from under the counter he announced, 'Well, the least I can do is open a fresh bottle for you boys.' After rapidly filling three glasses, he continued with, 'And don't pay me no mind. We're all a bit jumpy around here, what with two desperados holed up in the livery and a certain maniac on the loose out there with some kind of buffalo gun.'

As Henry and Kyle exchanged startled glances, Clemens smoothly replied, 'Wouldn't want to meet up with him then. All I've got is this old Schofield.' Even as he spoke, his right hand abruptly streaked down to pat the butt of the well-worn weapon. That action was enough to drain the colour from the saloon-keeper's face. Clemens chuckled as he threw the whiskey down his throat. 'That's pretty good stuff, barkeep.' Turning to the Timmons brothers, he noticed that they were deep in thought and had barely touched theirs. 'You see a finish to those?' the assassin forcefully enquired.

Startled, they both gulped down the strong liquor.

'Set them up again, bartender,' Clemens demanded. 'I was aiming to bed down in the livery, if I can find it in all this snow. Will I have anything to fear from these *desperados*?'

A scrawny fellow in a black frock coat spoke up from across the smoke-filled room. 'My name's Doctor Curren. I've been seeing to their injuries and I'd say they've got quite enough to worry about at the minute. If you walk soft, I'm sure they won't bother you.'

Clemens chuckled. 'Obliged to you, Doc. All I want is a quiet life.' Turning to the brothers, he went on, 'I'm about tuckered out, fellas. I'm going to head over to the stables and get some shuteye. Where are they, anyhow? You couldn't see a barn door in front of your face out there!'

The two freighters were quite obviously struggling with mixed emotions. They could feel that there was something badly amiss, but their sluggish minds just couldn't latch on to it. If the marshal had been present, they would have confided in him, but he wasn't. Suddenly very keen to be rid of the bloodstained stranger, Kyle blurted out, 'It's directly across the street. Just keep walking and you won't miss it.'

Oblivious to the renewed tension, the bartender added, 'The owner's out of town at present. There's a young lad, name of Nathan, looking out for it. He's a bit slow, so don't pay him no mind.'

John Clemens drained his second glass and licked his lips appreciatively. 'Obliged. Oh, and that really is good sipping whiskey. Your regulars must truly enjoy drinking here.' With that he winked slyly, turned away and made for the door. Nobody had made mention of a female arriving in town, but that was of no account. When he'd attended to business, he would find her and settle matters one way or another.

As he stepped out on to the street, the blizzard hit him like a wall. A biting wind tore into him and it was all he could do to stay upright. Shielding his eyes, Clemens braced himself and thrust forward. The rudimentary thoroughfare was a sea of white, which should have helped in a town without any form of street lighting, but so fierce was the storm that he could no longer make out a single building. It was also the reason that he missed the huge figure of Marshal Tunstall, as that individual ploughed up to the saloon door.

In all his years, Clemens had never experienced such a tempest. His weathered face stung from the snow's biting impact. He knew that he would have had a hard time of it out on the plains. To avoid colliding with his destination, he plodded on with his left arm outstretched until at last his gloved hand connected with something solid. In the lee of the building, the wind eased slightly, but even so he felt it best to hug the timber wall. After shifting to his left a few paces, he reached one of the main doors. Drawing his revolver, the man hunter beat on the door for a moment before easing it open slightly.

'Nathan,' he bellowed out. 'Lend a hand here. The lady sent me over with some vittles for the wounded, but it's blowing worse than a blue norther out here. I can't even get the god damn door open.' With that, he let the door slam shut and stepped to one side. Despite the atrocious conditions, a smile of anticipation spread across his hard features. Somebody was about to get one hell of a shock!

★   ★   ★

'He said he was searching for his wife, but since arriving here he hasn't even

mentioned her. Don't that seem odd?'
Kyle asked of the frowning lawman.

'Just where is he now?' Jared demanded.

'Said he was going to the stables for
some shuteye.'

The marshal grunted and rubbed a
meaty hand over his face. 'What iron
was he toting?'

'Just a revolver, but he left a saddle
and some belongings on our wagon,'
Henry helpfully volunteered.

'Go get them, now!'

'But, Marshal, it ain't fit for man nor
beast out there,' Kyle protested.

Jared leaned forward until he was
almost nose-to-nose with the startled
freighter. 'I know. That's why *you're*
going and I'm staying here in the
warmth. You brought this son of a bitch
into my town and now I need to find
out just who he is.'

★　★　★

After only a short delay, the heavy door
opened. Nathan, young and seemingly

222

permanently bewildered, poked his head out into the raging blizzard and recoiled slightly. The conditions were so fierce that he couldn't even see anybody and so, very reluctantly, he stepped outside.

As the door closed behind their reluctant young host, Taw Johnson glanced sharply over at his companion. He could hear the wind whistling outside, but that wasn't what bothered him. The two men were comfortably ensconced in the hayloft, only too happy to be under cover on such a dreadful night, but the outlaw boss never completely relaxed his guard.

'Get over here and cock your piece,' he barked. 'Something just ain't right down there.' So saying, he drew his revolver and crawled awkwardly over to the edge of the boarding. Dust and bits of hay showered down to the dirt floor below. Horses in some of the stalls began to stir uneasily, as if they too sensed something amiss.

★ ★ ★

As Nathan's vision adjusted slightly, he suddenly noticed, off to his left, a grim-faced individual holding a gun. The impressionable young man's eyes opened wide, like saucers. Thoroughly alarmed, he squawked, 'I don't know you!'

'Ditto,' was the baffling response.

'And you said you'd brought food,' the young man continued petulantly.

John Clemens surged forward. 'I lied!' he stated coldly and then rapped the barrel of his Schofield up against the side of Nathan's skull.

The blow was just sufficient to inject an uncomfortable blend of pain and fear into the young man. As tears welled up in his eyes, his assailant roughly yanked him around, so that he was abruptly facing the stables. Clemens spoke clearly into Nathan's left ear. 'You try to run or shout any warnings and you won't see another sunrise. Savvy?'

As the terrified youngster nodded, he was suddenly shoved towards the door. 'And where are those two tarnal cockchafers hiding?'

Nathan gulped. He'd never heard such words before, but their meaning was apparent, even to him. 'Up in the hayloft,' he blurted out. 'I don't think they're very nice men. Just like you.'

'Huh, reckon you're just about to find that out, sonny,' the terrifying stranger muttered. Then he jabbed his gun muzzle into the small of Nathan's back and barked out, 'Get that door open!'

Up in the hayloft, Jed groaned and reluctantly joined his leader. His splinted leg was throbbing like the devil and he just wanted to be left alone.

'Now what's occurring? I'm beginning to wish we'd stayed in Canada,' he grumbled. 'At least it was only the law that used to hunt us up there!'

'Shut up and watch the door,' his leader snarled. 'That little shit's up to something!'

At that very moment there was movement at the main entrance and the two men aimed their revolvers.

★ ★ ★

Marshal Tunstall unrolled the blanket and peered at the rifle and bandoliers in utter dismay. Of all those in the saloon, he alone immediately grasped their significance. 'Sweet Jesus, it's him!'

'Him what?' queried the barkeeper grumpily. He was aggrieved at the scratch that the Sharps had made on his tabletop.

Jared glanced wide-eyed at the others. His habitual calm had momentarily deserted him. 'The bastard that killed those two men. He's here to finish the job and by all accounts he's the very devil!'

As his words sank in, all eyes turned to the livery . . . except that of course no one had a hope of actually seeing the building. The bartender paled, as he recalled the disagreement over the quality of the house whiskey. 'Oh shit,' he mumbled.

The big lawman drew in a deep breath to steady himself. 'Ain't that the truth?' he retorted. His composure was returning and yet with it came real fear. It was a long time since he'd had to face up to such an obviously capable man killer. Unfortunately, as he kept telling everyone, Roy was his town and it was no longer just worthless border trash who were in grave danger. He had a clear duty to protect young Nathan . . . if he still lived! There was also another consideration. He turned to the diminutive figure of Doc Curren.

'Doc, I need you to get over to McLean's. Tell Cathy that no matter how much gunfire she hears, she's to stay put. She'll recognize you from the livery, so she should listen.'

The medical man had the wit and good grace to do as he was asked without complaint. He was barely out of the door before Jared drew his Remington and followed on. Pausing at the threshold, the lawman suddenly turned to the two freighters. Of all those present, they were probably most used to handling firearms.

'Get your scatterguns from the wagon and follow me to the stables.'

The brothers were aghast. 'This ain't our fight,' Henry protested. 'We're just here bringing supplies.'

'What you *brought* is that assassin into my town. If you want to carry on doing business here, you'll do as I say. Now move!' Then, without a backward glance, the part-time marshal stepped out of the building and disappeared into the swirling snowstorm.

★ ★ ★

As the heavy door swung open, Nathan lurched forward. His matted hair was coated with snow and he would normally have been relieved to return to his domain, but instead he was absolutely petrified.

'For pity's sake, don't shoot,' he

wailed at anyone who might be listening, but it was already too late.

Up in the hayloft, two six-guns blasted out simultaneously. One bullet ripped into his right arm, whilst the other neatly broke his collarbone. The fact that neither projectile was immediately life threatening had nothing to do with any finer feelings, but rather because both Taw and Jed had been aiming at the man crouching behind Nathan. Before the poor lad even had time to crumble to his knees, Clemens barged past him and raced underneath the hayloft.

As he passed below the scavengers' last location, he fired rapidly three times and then kept on moving to the rear of the stables. He well knew that all the gunfire would be likely to attract unwelcome attention and that he would probably need an ally, although that was highly unlikely to come in human form. Ears ringing, he dropped down inside a vacant stall and bellowed out, 'You slack-jawed faggots can't shoot worth a damn!'

Only one of his enemies was able to

respond to that. Jed, sorely hampered by his broken leg, had been unable to shift position rapidly enough and now lay dead from a bullet through his heart. Cursing fluently, Taw darted over to him and grabbed Jed's smoking revolver. With only his right arm functioning, he placed the spare Colt in the folds of his sling and yelled back, 'Maybe so, but I managed to take your woman away from you, didn't I?'

Clemens had more sense than to continue the fruitless exchange and so the only sound was Nathan's shrill screaming, as the youngster lay help-lessly on the floor near the entrance. That was how Jared found him when he cautiously pushed open one of the doors.

'God damn,' he muttered angrily. Although it was far from clear just who had actually shot the lad, John Clemens was now very definitely the town's problem and the lawman would need all the help he could get. 'You still alive in there, Johnson?' he yelled.

'Sure am,' Taw replied, as he carefully prowled around the hayloft. A moving target was always harder to hit. 'Jed's shot to hell, though. Clemens is at the back somewhere, hiding in a stall.'

'Then it seems like your enemy is now my enemy,' the marshal countered. 'But don't think this is over when he's dead, because you're as much to blame for this bloodbath as anyone.'

At that moment and much to his surprise, the Timmons brothers arrived, dutifully carrying their sawn-off shotguns. Nathan's wailing was audible even over the storm and they looked far from happy to be there. Jared gave them no time to reflect on their situation.

'Give me one of those scatterguns and some shells,' he demanded. 'The stable hand has taken a couple of bullets. Once I get in there, you'll have to follow on and grab him. Get him back to the saloon for Doc Curren to work on. And keep your heads down. He ain't the only casualty in there and I don't want any more.'

Henry and Kyle nodded reluctantly. They had no taste for any involvement in vicious gunplay, but they were coated in freezing snow and their role would at least allow them to return to some warmth.

After checking the loads on his borrowed weapon, Roy's marshal pushed the heavy door further open. Taking in a deep breath to steady his nerves, he charged forward past Nathan's squirming figure and then dropped to the ground. From near the rear of the building a gun crashed out and he felt a blast of pressure from a near miss. Cursing, Jared aimed his shotgun and squeezed one trigger. There was a tremendous roar and a blast of lead shot peppered the far stall.

With a cloud of smoke obscuring the immediate area, he yelled at the entrance, 'Move, you slackers, or I'll turn this big gun on you!'

The two freighters gulped in perfect unison. 'Where's he shot?' Kyle replied.

'Arm and shoulder looks like,' Jared responded impatiently.

Henry glanced at his brother. 'Grab a leg each and run, yeah?'

Kyle nodded. 'I suppose.' Then he called out, 'Cover us, Marshal.'

As Jared unleashed the second barrel in Clemens's general direction, the Timmons leapt into the building and seized hold of Nathan's ankles. With scant regard for his condition, they turned and dragged him across the threshold and out into the street. The youngster's screaming reached a new crescendo and then abruptly ceased. Mercifully, the increased pain had tipped him into unconsciousness, allowing the two men to carry him off through the blizzard without incident.

Although grateful for Nathan's removal, Jared knew that he wouldn't see the brothers again until, one way or another, it was all over. With the shotgun reloaded, he called up to the hayloft, 'If we're going to flush this bastard out, you need to get down here where you can do some good, savvy?'

Taw had been thinking along the same lines. With the loft stretching over the rear of the building, he was relatively safe from attack, but didn't have a shot at Clemens. The problem was that he had to get down the wooden ladder one handed, without taking a bullet. He was just about to find out that that would be the least of his worries!

13

The town marshal obviously knew his business, Clemens reflected and a sawn-off shotgun in the right hands was a truly terrifying weapon. To settle both his opponents, he would have to play dirty, but that had never troubled him in the past. With the stable containing a lot of nervous horses and one of the men somewhere above him, fire seemed like a useful ally. And there were plenty of lit kerosene lamps conveniently dotted about the timber building.

Glancing around his refuge, the assassin spotted a pitchfork impaled in a bale of hay. If he was going to make a move, it had to be before the last outlaw dropped down from the loft and joined in. Holstering his revolver, Clemens scrabbled over to the vicious implement. He hefted it in his hand to test the balance and then hurled it with all his strength towards the lawman.

As the deadly prongs arced towards him, Jared reacted fast. After rolling twice, he fired once at the stall, but his target was already on the move. Clemens swiftly reached the nearest lamp. It was hanging from a hook next to a pile of leather tackle. Quickly removing the cap on the fuel reservoir, he pitched the whole thing over to the base of the wooden ladder with uncanny accuracy. Even as the glass shattered and the kerosene flared into life, the relentless assassin was already shifting position again . . . but this time he only just made it.

The shotgun crashed out once more and at last some of the pellets ripped through flesh and blood. The pain was such that he was quite unable to stifle a howl. With part of his left ear torn away and a piece of lead agonizingly lodged in the nape of his neck, Clemens again raced for the rear of the stables.

Transferring the empty 'two shoot' gun to his left hand, the marshal drew and fired his Remington. Knowing the quality of the opponent that he was up against, he only fired a couple of shots. To empty both weapons without a definite kill would be to leave himself at the other man's mercy.

As the fugitive dived for cover in another empty stall, the frustrated lawman could see that everything had suddenly changed. The livery was on fire and there were at least twenty terrified horses kicking out at their wooden enclosures. Saving the animals had to be his priority. His personal attraction to Cathy could no longer count.

'Why don't you just take your wife and go?' he bellowed. 'There's been more than enough killing!'

The answer, when it finally came, was far from encouraging. 'Nobody takes what's mine and lives to brag about it! Besides, you've made me bleed and now you're going to pay!'

Jared sighed. It was just his luck to come up against someone who lived by the feud! He glanced up to find Johnson peering over the side of the loft. Flames, fed by the abundance of dry straw, were leaping up both the ladder and the wall at its side. The rope and pulley was available, but that came with its own dangers.

'If you want to live, you'll need to shimmy down that rope. Or better still, just jump, 'cause you can be sure that bastard'll be waiting. When you hit the ground, roll and stay low. I'll try to cover you, but make it quick.'

Taw stared nervously at the long drop for a moment. Swinging down a rope with only one good arm wasn't an option, but he could at least sit on the edge to reduce the distance. Choking from the smoke, the outlaw got on to his backside and lowered his legs over the side.

'Jump, god damn it,' the marshal urged.

Even as he toppled forward, a gun crashed out and Taw felt a shocking pain in his left leg. He didn't even hear the shotgun triggered in response, because rather than landing and rolling as intended, he hit the hard packed dirt with punishing force and immediately lost consciousness.

'That's just great,' Jared muttered bleakly. Now he was all alone against a gun-crazed maniac in a burning building full of panicked horses.

Cathy remained immobile for one full minute after Doc Curren's departure, as she considered his message. Then the young woman eased open the door and stepped out into the freezing tumult. Ignoring the buffeting, she listened in horror to the muffled gunfire. Like it or not, her future existence revolved around the fate of the three men across the street, because she had sense enough to realize that a woman alone on the frontier was easy pickings. Without money, the best that she could hope for was a gruelling and short life of prostitution. It was this depressing knowledge that meant she had to ignore the marshal's instructions and force herself out into the raging blizzard.

The wooden steps were coated in snow and at the bottom the makings of a drift awaited her. Once through that the going became a little easier, because the power of the wind was literally blasting the fresh snow off the street and up against the buildings. Cathy knew the sound of thunder when she heard it, man-made or otherwise. Taking short, sharp steps she soon covered the distance. Before her loomed the massive stable doors, but there was something else as well. Deep inside the structure, a flickering glow was visible through the minute gaps in the timber planking. The building was on fire and there wasn't a soul around to help.

The flames had the wooden structure in a death grip and no bucket chain on earth was going to douse them. All Jared could hope to do was save the animals without getting himself killed in the process. But how could he possibly open the double doors without being shot in the back? Then, as if heaven sent, he felt a blast of cold air and turned to see Cathy's lovely but anxious features at the threshold. The wind fanned the fire, but it mattered not. The livery was doomed anyway.

'Get those doors open,' he shouted. 'I've got to get the horses out of here.' He didn't mention the fact that he would most probably have to kill her husband in the process.

Breaking the shotgun, Jared replaced the cartridges and then cautiously moved towards the terrified animals. As first one door and then the next opened, the flames intensified so that the heat on his face was almost intolerable. If Johnson didn't wake up soon the outlaw would be toast, but it was John Clemens that concerned him most. The assassin had been strangely inactive for a while.

Reaching the first stall, the lawman kicked the thick pole from its mountings and was rewarded by the crazed beast lunging past him and off out into the night. Then he moved rapidly from stall to stall, all the time keeping the shotgun trained on his last sighting of the gunman. As more and more horses fled to safety, he began to think that he might just pull it off.

Bizarrely, in spite of the terrible danger, it suddenly occurred to him that when it was all over he really ought to hand in his badge and stick to blacksmithing, because carrying the law in such a spineless town was a completely thankless task. The thought brought a grim smile to his flushed and sweaty features.

Clemens could hear the released horses pounding away, so he knew that the marshal must be getting closer, but the pain in the back of his neck was so intense that he simply couldn't focus. The piece of metal lodged there had to be touching a nerve, because it was all he could do not to cry out. Dropping to his knees, he knew that it was time to take drastic measures.

Withdrawing his knife from its

sheath, he reached up and positioned the point next to the entry wound. Then, because he had no illusions about what was to come, he put the leather cover between his teeth and tightly clenched them. Next he placed his left forefinger over the entry wound, so as to guide the narrow blade in. Drawing in a stream of super-heated air through his nostrils, he abruptly held his breath and eased in the vicious probe.

A fresh wave of agony swept over him, but this wasn't the first time that John Clemens had operated on himself. Fighting back the nausea and with sweat pouring off his face, he dug deeper until finally the knife point reached under the lead shot. His right hand was trembling, but there was far worse to come. Because the blade would not bend, he had to penetrate deeper before pivoting it upwards. As the existing wound was torn wider, the pain was indescribable. Suddenly over-whelmed by a peculiar sense of detachment, the gunman acknowledged that he was going to faint and most probably burn to d . . .

With an unexpected surge, the blood-coated pellet burst out and was lost in the hay. Unable to control a muffled groan, Clemens fell forward and lay doubled over for a long moment. But then the frenzied movement of more animals signified Marshal Tunstall's relentless approach and he spat out the sheath. That god damned law dog was going to pay!

The flames had nearly spread across one entire wall, but with only a couple of horses left to free, Jared had high hopes of being able to slip out of the small door at the rear. His skin felt like parchment in the intense heat and he longed to roll in the freezing snow. Unfortunately, the next fear-maddened beast was directly opposite an apparently empty stall and he was by no means certain that his deadly foe was incapacitated. Levelling his shotgun, the marshal momentarily averted his gaze as he kicked out sideways at the sliding pole. The trapped animal was in a frenzy of terror, with blood shot eyes and bleeding flanks. Suddenly liberated, the creature instinctively surged forward towards the open doors.

It was at that moment that John Clemens's buckskin clad form leapt from the semi-darkness. His revolver fired what should have been the kill shot. The bullet struck the careering horse in its neck, but such was its momentum that it was past Jared in an instant. As the gunman desperately cocked his weapon, his badly abused neck convulsed and he swayed slightly. That momentary respite allowed Jared to transfer his gaze and line up the shotgun.

Squeezing the first trigger, he felt the comforting recoil as the twelve-gauge cartridge detonated. The blast caught Clemens squarely in his chest and threw him back into the rear wall of the stall. Peering at his nemesis in stunned disbelief, the stricken assassin tried to raise his right hand by sheer strength of will. Without any hesitation, Jared fired again and watched with horrified relief as the other man's disfigured, blood-spattered body absorbed the deadly projectiles and collapsed on to the hay.

The marshal was riveted to the spot for a long moment, before he suddenly blinked and came to his senses. The building was fast becoming a blazing inferno. Even the loft above him was ablaze. He could feel the skin on his face beginning to blister. Without even time to reload, he raced to the final stall. Slamming the solid pole to one side, Jared stepped back as the maddened creature charged past. A mere two yards further on was a water barrel and then the rear door. He had made it.

But then he recalled Taw Johnson, lying near the main entrance. Although the man was most probably dead, there was always the slim chance that he wasn't. 'God damn it,' he cursed. Dashing over to the barrel, he thrust his head deep into the soothing liquid and then turned away to run the length of the doomed building. The fatally wounded horse had collapsed on its side. Unwilling to let the poor creature burn to death, he paused to shoot it in the head with his Remington before moving on.

Cathy Clemens had remained outside, trembling in splendid isolation as, one by one, the escaping horses had charged past into the night. Not one member of the community had come to investigate and assist their part-time marshal, which said a lot about Roy's citizens. With the storm still raging, they were probably not even aware that the livery was on fire, but no one could have been oblivious to the confrontation taking place.

More shooting broke out at the rear of the stables and the young woman finally overcame her fear and tentatively entered the building. She barely escaped being trampled by another panicked animal and then peered around in sheer disbelief. Tongues of flame danced in the rafters above and the burning heat hit her like a wall. The snow on her head was gone in an instant and she couldn't believe that anyone could survive in such conditions. Then, unbelievably, she caught sight of the huge marshal pounding towards her.

As he stopped next to a wounded horse, a sudden movement caught her attention off to the right. Taw Johnson, with fresh blood coating his left leg, was struggling to get to his feet. Her natural instinct was to rush forward and help him, but something stopped her. The sole remaining outlaw was staring intently at Roy's marshal. As the mercy shot rang out, Johnson's right hand dropped to his holster . . . only to find it empty. When tumbling from the hayloft with another gunshot wound, the revolver had leapt from his grasp and ended up mere feet from where Cathy was standing. Blissfully unaware of her presence, the sole remaining scavenger watched as Jared moved rapidly towards him. That man's features were dripping with a mixture of sweat and water. He was close to collapse from heat exhaustion and so didn't notice Johnson until they were about three yards apart.

'You look like a scorched turd, Marshal,' came the colourful greeting.

Jared came to a shuddering stop and regarded the other man with bewildered surprise.

'I thought you were a goner for sure,' he commented.

'It takes a lot to kill me,' Taw returned. 'I take it that poxy man hunter's finally mustered out.'

Jared nodded wearily. 'Deader than a wagon tyre.'

The outlaw raised his eyebrows and nodded. The heat was intolerable, but he showed no inclination to move. 'Then you did good. Real good. That cockchafer's been haunting me for days. He was something special, in a sick kind of way.' He paused momentarily. His eyes never left the lawman. 'Well, I guess I'd better get this leg fixed up and then we'll be on our way. By we, I mean Cathy and me.'

Having already noticed Johnson's

empty holster, the marshal slowly shook his head. There was far more than just the atrocious weather on his mind.

'Don't ask me why, but I only came back here to see if you were still alive. Since you are, you ain't going anywhere until I find out just who shot Nathan. If he clears you, that's fine. If not, then you'll be facing charges.'

Taw smiled, but the apparent good will completely failed to reach his eyes. 'I kind of thought you might say that.' So saying, he quickly reached into the folds of his sling and with a flourish produced Jed's revolver. Cocking it, he levelled it at the lawman and remarked, 'I've seen enough bad men in my time to recognize a good one. So believe me when I say I'll regret this . . . but not enough not to do it.'

Holding only an empty shotgun and taken completely by surprise, Jared's sole defence consisted of words. 'If you gun me down, it'll be obvious that you did it, because I'm nowhere near Clemens's body. And in your condition, there's no way you'd be able to just hightail it out of town.'

Taw shook his head regretfully. 'Nice try, Marshal, but by morning this place will be just ashes. Your precious citizens will be lucky to even find your belt buckle. Nobody will know who did what.'

From over near the door, a female voice startled them both. 'I'll know!'

Both men twitched with surprise, but only one of them was in a position to react. Wincing from the pain in his blood-soaked leg, Taw shuffled to his right, all the while keeping his gun on the lawman. Finally, he was able to observe Cathy with his peripheral vision. His glance took in the cocked revolver in her hand, although he had no idea that it was actually his.

'Well, well. You're getting pretty good at sneaking up on people. But you know, the best thing you can do is point that iron somewhere else and leave me to it. Or, come to think of it, you could shoot this law dog yourself. After all, he has just killed your devoted husband!'

Cathy shook her head adamantly. 'I can't let you do it. He's a better man than you'll ever live to be.'

The outlaw smiled knowingly. 'Ah, so it's like that, is it? And not even a tear for poor John Clemens. It seems you've got some hard bark on you, Cathy girl, but I don't think there's enough to stop me doing what I need to.'

With that, he returned all his attention to the man before him. As his forefinger tightened, he remarked grimly, 'See you in hell, Marshal!'

As the shot crashed out, Jared's body jerked uncontrollably. He had steeled himself against the inevitable agony and yet remarkably none came. Instead it was the outlaw who swayed under the punishing impact of a bullet. Taw Johnson stared at him in amazement.

'I never thought she'd do it,' he finally managed. His gun hand had wavered and now he made one last supreme effort to get it back on track.

Even as Jared bellowed out, 'Leave him, Cathy,' he hurled the empty

252

shotgun at the mortally wounded scavenger and drew his own revolver. Thumbing back the hammer, he fired and then rapidly repeated the action. The two bullets smashed into Johnson's chest and pitched him backwards. The dying outlaw, torso coated in blood, twitched violently and then lay still. Jared stood over him for a moment, shaking his head. He was suddenly aware that Cathy had joined him.

'I'm glad his kind don't all take five bullets to put down,' he commented. 'Marshalling is tough enough as it is.' Then he holstered his Remington and placed a hand on her arm. 'Thanks for that. Oh, and I'm sorry about your husband, but he really didn't leave me any choice.'

She gazed up into his eyes and favoured him with a sad smile. 'I know. He wasn't an easy man to live with . . . any more than Taw would have been, I suppose. One of these days I might get it right, but for now can we please just get out of here before I burn to death?'

With the sudden release of tension, Jared abruptly realized just how appalling the heat was. Grabbing Timmons's shotgun, he followed her out of the blazing livery. The ferocious chill almost took their breath away, but for a few moments the blizzard was actually a blessed relief. And quite remarkably there wasn't a single soul on the street.

'God damn chickens,' he shouted over the wind. 'They all want the law, but when it comes to a shooting, they're no help at all!'

Keeping the young woman under his lee, he shepherded her over to the saloon. As the two of them burst into the gentle warmth, Jared regarded the assembled citizens scornfully. Tossing the well used sawn-off to one of the startled freighters, he contemptuously remarked, 'In case you sons of bitches hadn't noticed, there's a fire to fight over there!'

14

The new day brought with it a bizarre sight in the town of Roy, Montana. The hellish wind had dropped, leaving nearly the whole settlement coated in thick snow. The exception was of course the livery stables, or rather, the vast expanse of smoking ashes that were all that remained of it. Almost the whole population stood around the site, soaking up the tremendous residual heat. It was the first time many of them had been properly warm since the summer.

As Jared and Cathy came out of the eating house after breakfast, he chuckled grimly. 'Look at them all. They didn't want to go near the damn place last night. If they'd had anything about them, they could have salvaged some timber for their own stoves.'

Carefully scrutinizing his surroundings as he always did, the lawman noticed that Henry and Kyle Timmons had eschewed the temporary heat source. Having dragged off the snow covered tarpaulin, they were working hard at unloading their wagons. Only once the contents were in McLean's store would they get paid. The freighters felt his hard stare, but kept their eyes averted.

Jared's face was red raw and he was sorely tempted to daub it with axle grease. The only thing preventing him was the effect it might have on Cathy. Because the one good feature that had come from the unexpected outbreak of bloody violence was her presence in town. Jared's problem was that he was unsure how to advance his cause. For all his size and practical abilities, he had never found it easy to interact with the fairer sex. He was about to stumble into an opening gambit when she suddenly made matters a lot easier for him.

'Why didn't you want me to finish Taw off?'

With such a subject, the marshal was on firmer ground. Regarding her searchingly, he replied, 'I'm guessing that you've never killed anyone before. It's a hell of a thing to take a man's life. It stays with you for a long time. I just wanted to save you from that.'

With no one around to intrude, Cathy turned to face him and gently placed her hands on his shoulders. 'You're a good man, Jared Tunstall. I sensed that the first time we met. My problem is that I've always got involved with the wrong sort. I just never seem to get it right.'

A surge of hope welled up inside him and he almost did a jig in the slush. Then reality intruded and he came down to earth with a crash. 'Well, I've tried to lead a decent life and probably because of that I haven't got much to offer. This town doesn't usually need and certainly doesn't deserve a good lawman and as the blacksmith, all I've got is a shack at the back of the smithy.'

She looked up into his eyes and much to his surprise, favoured him with a delightful laugh. 'Perhaps you should try your hand at ranching. There just happens to be a small spread up near Chinook that's very recently had its owner die. It's called New Haven and it could be the chance for a fresh start for the both of us.'

Jared gazed at her in amazement. 'You'd take such a risk? You've only known me for two days.'

The young woman smiled. 'Likewise. But by the time we get up there in this weather it'll seem like a lifetime and if we've had enough of each other by then . . . well, this town will still need a blacksmith.'

Unable to contain his pleasure, Jared seized her in a bear hug. The future was definitely looking up. Although tightly enveloped in his arms, Cathy nevertheless managed to add, 'And there'll be another consolation if it doesn't work out, because you'll also be the owner of a well maintained Sharps rifle!' With that, she winked at him and he suddenly knew that everything was going to be all right.